ANITBEET PRO... MW00973964

Obsessive

Intimacies

A Novel by *Yani*

Sex, Secrets, Lies & Obsession. Markel and Tierra have it all; great careers, money, stability, love and most importantly; a family. But when troubles on the inside become knowledge to the wrong people on the outside, secret affairs quickly turn into a deadly obsession.

Yani

A Note from Yani

This is my first erotic novel and boy, was it an experience! My first three novels, the Amazon Best Selling series *A Thug's Redemption*, was a mixture of urban fiction with lots of suspense, comedy and a thrill ride from start to finish. I enjoyed writing all three books to that series, however, I really wanted to take a chance and step away from my comfort zone.

I started *Obsessive Intimacies* when I was 18 years old and pregnant with my daughter. At the time, I believe that I was too young and too inexperienced to write such a book, which is why eleven years later, it is just now seeing its completion. I think my novel will be relatable to many women who have been cheated on but stayed with their spouse while keeping quiet and women who have been cheated on and stayed, but couldn't help getting payback- the age old "what's good for the goose" ideology. Some of the questions that Tierra asks are many questions women, including myself, are asking every day. "Why do men cheat?" "What is wrong with me?" "How come I'm not enough?" As women, we know the answer to these questions, it's just hard for us to admit to this answer. We come up with various excuses, but the truest answer will always remain the same. Men cheat because we allow them too. That's the bottom line. We will go through the motions of trying to wait for him to mature, wait for him to commit and the biggest mistake of all, we try to change the man. A woman will change herself before she is successful in changing her man.

I am glad that I waited until I experienced life a little more and all that comes with it; joy, pain, heartache, and sorrow, because it allowed me to write this book from the heart and make this story as real and enjoyable (and JUICY) as I possibly could. So this book is dedicated both to the women who have been cheated on, the women who had the courage to leave, the women who stayed because of their faith in their partners, and the men who just can't keep their #@!& in their pants. I hope you all enjoy. Peace!

1

Markel

The sound of my alarm clock screeching like a
Freight train straining to come to a halt blared in my ears
and snatched me out of my dream, which was actually a
pretty good one. I was back in my undergrad days, living
the good and wild life, getting any lady that I wanted,
being a pimp; hated by the brothers who wished they
could be me, and loved and lusted after by the women
that wished they could get a taste of the mojo I was
always laying on them. Ahh yes, I was indeed the
definition of a player. But now, those days are dead and
gone, and I am a one woman man. My wife, my boo, my
right hand lady Tierra, has stayed with me in spite of all
of my in-discretions. Sometimes I wonder if she knew
about all of the cheating and the double life I was leading
with her and my side "jawns", but just kept her mouth

Yani

closed. Maybe she even got a little on the side. No, I'm not going to think that. Even though I did my dirt, I don't even want to think of the possibility of another man running up in my wife. I would have to murder something.

Now I'm looking at her sleeping beside me. Damn, she is truly beautiful. No matter how many women I had that would have done anything- and I do mean anything- to be with me, I knew it was only because I was popular and they smelled success. Those bitches were just trying to hitch on and get a free ride. But Tierra, she is real and is loyal. She is the definition of what a 100 percent woman truly is supposed to be: smart, beautiful, a great conversationalist, and a great cook. I mean, my baby can really throw down! She has her own catering business and was just contracted to do a cook book as well as do a cooking segment on Rachel Ray's Morning Show. Yes, my baby is the bomb diggity. Did I mention this woman has some toe curling cuddy? After almost 16 years, this woman still manages to surprise me in bed and leave me glowing like a newly fucked virgin, grinning from ear to ear, drooling, and wondering all at the same time, DAMN!!! Where the hell did she learn how to do that?!

And to think that I almost screwed everything up with her, running around, sticking and moving with a bunch of smuts that didn't have half of what Tierra has. I'm just looking at her right now laying on her side, back arched, silk sheets clinging to her curvy body outlining that sexy frame that still looks tight after giving birth to our three beautiful kids. Damn, the way that ass of hers is pointing in my direction is making me want to slob her down right now! Damn, my baby is fine! I love her to death. I really don't know what I would do without her.

I can hear the kids up. It sounds like Tamia and Tianna are going at it again. Those girls stay going at it. And here comes one knocking on the door.

"Daddy!!" That was Tianna. She's ten years old but is such a Tom boy and swears she's a little boxer, though I must admit, she has a mean right hook and has made me want to cry uncle when she punched me in my damned eye. I was almost ready to whip her little ass.

"Yes sweetheart," I replied while placing my hands behind my head, knowing what was coming next.

Without getting permission from me, Tianna burst open my door, marched into my bedroom, and placed her hands on her tiny hips as she took a defiant stance.

That was her "I'm sick of this shit" pose. I managed to suppress my chuckle and asked her what was wrong.

She rolled her eyes and started tapping her foot. I almost cracked up. "Tamia has been in the shower for the last half hour washing her hair AGAIN, and I have to go to the bathroom."

Now I had to roll my eyes. Tamia. That girl. Every time I turn around she is taking forever in the damn day to get herself ready in the morning. She just turned thirteen and thinks she is Miss Body Beautiful. She has long, dark-brown hair just like her mother. The same almond shaped, baby brown eyes; thick, naturally arched eye brows, long lashes, and smooth, sandy-brown skin. And unfortunately, puberty has begun to kick in a little sooner than I would have liked because she has to be sporting at least a 34B with a little tiny waist and a little apple bottom. As her father, I naturally am ready to pull a Martin Lawrence from Bad Boys 2 and intimidate any little nucca that thinks he is going to smooth talk his way into my baby girl's pants. I was thirteen once, too and I can't even begin to tell you the filthy thoughts that would have been running through my mind had Tamia grown

up with me and my little crew of cronies. Yeah… I
definitely was going to be keeping a hawk-eye on her.

I guess I didn't answer her fast enough because
Tianna started tapping her foot louder.

"Daddy, did you hear me?" she asked impatiently.
"Tell her to get out of the bathroom. I've gotta go!" She
crossed her legs and started doing the "pee-pee" dance
to drive her point home. I got off the bed and let her use
our master bathroom and then decided to handle Miss
America.

I tapped on the bathroom door.

"I said wait, DANG!!" Tamia hollered from behind
the door.

"Who the hell do you think you're talking to like
that?" I shouted back. I heard her wince behind the
door.

"Sorry, daddy. I thought you were Tianna again. She
knows I'm in here trying to get ready for school." I could
just see her rolling her eyes while she did whatever the
hell it was that she was doing to her head.

"Regardless who you thought it was, you don't yell
in my house. Get your little scrawny ass out the
bathroom. You're not the only one that has to go to

school." I could hear her sucking her teeth as she snatched her things up in the bathroom. Though her words weren't exactly audible, I knew she was talking shit.

"You say something?" I challenged her.

"No, Daddy," she mumbled. Yeah, she knows who the boss is. She cracked the door open and peeked out. I scanned over her and noticed how unusually short her uniform skirt was. I shook my head. You can't even send your kids to Catholic School to keep them in line. They always gotta push the envelope... even with Jesus.

"What the hell is wrong with your skirt?" I asked her.

She looked down at herself and gave me the dumb blonde look as though she had no idea what I was talking about. "What do you mean?" she asked with wide, innocent eyes.

"Where is the rest of it?"

She chuckled and threw her hand on my chest. "Dad, you're silly."

"You see me damn it laughing? Ether you have Tianna's uniform on or you need to pull your skirt down.

9

Either way, don't play yourself. Pull that damn skirt down."

She sulked past me and whined, "Aww Dad, come on. It's not even that high. It looks corny all the way past my knees."

"Yeah and you look like Steve Urkel with the hem of your skirt around your collar bone. Pull that damn skirt down." I could tell she was embarrassed by my last comment, but oh well. She pulled her skirt down and her knee highs up before sulking towards her bedroom. "And put your hair in a ponytail. And don't even think about pulling your skirt back up when you get to school. I've got eyes everywhere. So even when you think I'm not looking, I still see you." I heard Tianna skipping down the hallway behind me.

"Ah ha!" she teased. "That's what you get for trying to be cute for them nappy-headed knuckle-heads that hang around the building in the morning and in the afternoon. Daddy, Tamia's trying to get a boyfriend." She leaned into the wall laughing and slapped her knee.

"Shut up, Tianna!" Tamia screamed from her bedroom.

Yani

"Who's the knuckle-head, Tee-Tee?" I asked my younger daughter as I chuckled with her.

"His name is Troy and he's ugmo," she whispered in between her laughs. I laughed out loud with her. Ugmo? Damn, my little girl was getting dolled up for a troll. Her mom was definitely going to have to school her.

Tamia snatched her door open. "You talk too much you little troll. I am not trying to get a boyfriend. I don't even like Troy. You need to mind your business."

"Hey, what did I just tell you about your mouth? You better chill real quick with your lip Tamia, or the only thing you'll be kissing is the back of your momma's hand." She closed her mouth quickly knowing Tierra did not play when it came to sassy mouthed little girls. "Now I don't give a damn who Troy is but you better stay outta his face and I better not catch him in yours, or I'll bust his ass and then I'ma bust yours. Don't let me hear anything else about you trying to wear your school uniform skirts a little shorter to get attention from some ugmo Negro." Tianna burst out laughing and Tamia rolled her eyes as she crossed her arms over her chest. "And that goes for you too, Smoking Joe." That was a little nick name that I gave my younger daughter since she has such a mean right hook.

"You don't have to worry, Daddy. Boys are the last thing on my mind. They're immature, simple and don't know nothing about nothing."

"That's right." I agreed as I gave my daughter a pound. "Go get ready for school. And wake your little brother up, too." I went back in the bedroom and saw that Tierra wasn't in the bed anymore. So much for my early morning jump off. Damned rugrats. I went into our master bathroom and saw that she was finishing brushing her teeth.

"Good morning, baby." I put my arms around her waist from behind and hugged her to me before kissing the side of her mouth. She turned her head a little to meet my mouth and gave me a big wet kiss. Then she handed me the toothpaste.

"Good morning, babe." She giggled. "Handle that."

"Oh, I see you got jokes early in the morning. You're trying to be funny." I snatched the toothpaste from her playfully.

"No I'm not. Your breath is just a little tart. That's not cute." She laughed out loud and made her way out of our bathroom. I slapped her on her ass playfully.

"Was that the girls going at it again?" Tierra asked from the bedroom as I was brushing my teeth.

I swished water around my mouth and then spat it in the toilet and flushed. "Yeah. We really need to do something about Tamia and her attitude. Her mouth is getting a little bit crazy in here and that bathroom situation is getting out of hand." I came in the bedroom and began taking my clothes out for work.

"I've told her about her mouth too many times. That girl's mouth is seriously about to get her a check that her ass can't cash."

I looked at my wife and laughed. I loved how she is such a lady with such an aggressive attitude and a foul mouth to match. "Well if her ass can't cash the checks, will your ass take some deposits?" We both laughed.

"You are so damned nasty. I'm going to cook breakfast. Are you eating here or picking something up on your way into the office?"

"I gotta pick Darnell up since his car is in the shop, so we might just grab something on our way in." I watched my wife walk out of the bedroom and head downstairs. I really am a lucky man.

2

Tierra

Markel has no idea how freaking lucky he is. I love that man to death, but he has not made it easy to do so. He has cheated, lied and Lord only knows what else during the duration of our relationship, which goes all the way back to 8th grade at Wannamaker Junior High School. Most people would say that I was stupid for staying with him, that I was and still am too good to deal with the bullshit that he was putting me through. But Eve said it best in her song lyrics: Love is blind, and it will take over your mind. I love Markel with everything I have inside of me, and even though those dingy bitches may have had him for a night or two, I have the ring, the house, the Range Rover, the money, the commitment and ultimately, the man. All they have are memories and thoughts of what could've been but never was. Besides, while he was doing his dirt on the side, I had my little action too. What's good for the goose is good for the damn gander and two can definitely play that game.

Obsessive Intimacies

As far as I can tell, Markel has been totally faithful since we had Tianna and got married. And so have I. He comes home on time, he calls when he is going to be late and he is totally devoted to making me and the kids happy as well as taking care of home. Besides, he would be a fool to fuck up now. My baby is the head Physical Therapist at one of the most prestigious clinics in the Tristate area. He has treated numerous athletes from Allen Iverson to Ocho-Cinco. My baby is well known and even sought after. So of course he is paid out of the ass making a six figure salary. But, as the saying goes: Hell hath no fury like a woman scorned... without a pre-nup. So he definitely knows better now.

Markel and I met when I moved from Atlanta to Philadelphia in the fall of 1996 when we were in the 8th grade. He was a little knuckle-head mofo with a crew of cronies that swore they were the next best thing since sliced bread. The boys in the class were immediately on my top because of my southern accent, curvy teenaged body and long, dark brown hair. But the females, those chicken-heads threw shade on me the moment my gorgeous ass walked through the doors.

Yani

I will never forget my first initial encounter with Markel. I had only been in school for about two weeks when one of the chicken-heads in the class figured she would test my gangsta. We were at lunch and they were jealous because my mother always sent me to school not only looking fresh, but with hot, home cooked food so I didn't have to eat the nasty school lunch. The boldest chicken-head tripped me as I was walking by sipping on my Pepsi and I stumbled, spilling my soda on the front of my new Ralph Lauren sweat suit.

Markel stood on top of the lunch table, laughed and shouted, "Check mate!"

Little Miss Chicken-Head had a crush on Markel and didn't like the fact that he and his boys were always trying to holler at me in school, so I guess she thought she would get his attention by dissing me. I had something special for that ass. I picked my bottle of Pepsi up, threw it in the trash and a couple of her friends decided to instigate. I walked over to Little Miss Chicken-Head and she stood up. I think she was about to say something but the words never made it out of that heifer's mouth because I knocked the shit out of that bitch. When she fell into the lunch table, I grabbed a carton of milk and poured it in her hair and her face and beat that ass. I was daring one of her little crew of sluts to jump into it because they would have gotten some of the same.

When security broke the fight up, Markel stood on top of the table over the girl and said in his best Chris Tucker/Smokey from the movie *Friday* voice: "YOU GOT KNOCKED THE FUCK OUT!!!" Reminiscing about that now almost has me cracking up at this sink as I'm fixing breakfast for my babies.

I sat in the counselor's office with an ice-pack on my hand more pissed off that I had just gotten that damned sweat suit and the bitch made me spill Pepsi on it, than the fact that I was about to be suspended and hadn't even been in the damn school for a month. Markel snuck into the counselor's office and just stood in front of me. I looked up at him and we stared each other down. As angry as I was, he actually made me blush. He must've known that he had me because he started grinning. That turned my smile into a grimace.

He burst out laughing and said, "You gonna knock me out, too?"

"Boy, get out of my damned face." I snarled at him.

"Ooh! You better watch your mouth. You're already in trouble," he replied as he sat next to me.

"So what. That's what that little cow gets for trying to test me." I rubbed the ice-pack across my fist.

Markel just stared me in my face like I was going to be on the next science test and he needed to study me.

"Your accent is tight," he complimented.

I turned around and looked at him but quickly looked away. I'd never noticed how cute he was until that moment. "Thank you," I mumbled.

"So look, right. My name is Charlie and I need a bodyguard. Will you be my Angel?" We both burst out laughing. That had to be the corniest but cutest line I had ever heard any guy use. I laughed so hard I almost forgot that I had messed up my new outfit and was about to be suspended. The Principal came into the office and looked at the both of us.

"Markel Davis if you don't get out of this office and make your way back to your last period class, you will find your tail on the end of one of these pink slips, too." The Principal chided. She called my boy by his first and last name so I knew he had made her acquaintance more than once.

"Alright Ms. Jackson, my whole government though," he joked. The look that she gave him let him know that she was not in a joking mood. "Okay, I'm going. But Tierra is my study partner so I figured if she is getting suspended, I might as well get her contact information to make sure she don't fall behind in the school work. We're about to have a test soon and she already started here late."

"Damn this boy has game for days," I thought to myself.

The Principal looked at him and then looked at me. I shrugged my shoulders and took a pen out of my bag and a piece of paper out of my book. I knew why he really wanted my number, but his suave nature was too much to resist. I scribbled my name and number down on the paper and gave it to him. He grinned like a cat that had just caught the canary and left the office. From that moment on, he was a constant thought on my mind. Little did I know, he would be the source of my heartache, the father of my children, but also the love of my life.

3

Darnell

"Yo Bro! Let's go. You know Mondays are always crazy busy and we got clients coming in today!" Markel shouted out of his window. Dude was always trying to cock block. I was trying to crack on a little shorty that was on her way into IHOP as we were on our way out. Shorty was looking right with her tight fitted jeans and Gucci boots with the matching bag. Nails done, hair done; oh yeah, she was fancy!

"Hold on dawg, I'm coming. Chill out!" I turned my attention back to the little honey dip and smiled. "He's just mad because he's on lock down and is missing out on the finer things in life like you," I smiled at her and gave her the once over look. She giggled and took out her android phone and put my number in it. I put her number in my iPhone and told her I would give her a call tonight so we could go out for dinner and maybe the comedy club. Kevin Hart was in town and there was no way I was going to miss that. As she turned to walk away,

21

I took a picture of her ass. It took everything I had inside of me to keep from hollering "DAMN!" I can't wait to hit that. I strolled back over to Markel's car. It glistened in the sunlight from being freshly washed and waxed. That 2012 Acura was the shit. He had mad bitches on his dick just because of the car. I still don't know why he sold out and got married. I mean, don't get me wrong, Tierra is cool and all, but she was just a school jawn and he should've left it at that. The only reason she got the ring is because she fucked around and got pregnant TWICE. Two rugrats just aren't enough for me to wife a bitch. And I still say ole dawg needs to get a DNA test for at least the first two. Because I'm pretty sure she had niggas creeping on the low while they were in school. She just always struck me as the sneaky bitch.

I hopped in the whip and threw my shades on once he pulled off and the sun started blaring in my eyes. "Yo, you were definitely in the way for that shit. You saw me trying to get with the little honey dip."

Markel leaned back in his leather seat and whipped the wheel around a turn with one hand. "Man, you can crack on any honey you want to dawg, but when clients are coming in for a tour of the facility to do business, you know I like to get in early to make sure everybody's shit is on point. Last thing I want to see are sloppy desks with a bunch of paper work and shit and patients' charts unorganized and not where they're supposed to be. As for your honey dip, you better check shorty's ID and make sure her shit's legit. I do not need my right hand man getting hauled off in handcuffs at the job. Shit is not good for business." We both cracked up laughing.

"You trying to play me, dude. Naw, shorty is cool. She's definitely something kinda spectacular."

"Yeah alright." Markel replied stopping at a red light. "All I'm saying is, you're getting up there in that age, don't you think it's time for you to settle down a bit. You can't be a pimp forever." Markel is my home-boy but he gets on my fucking nerves trying to talk me into settling down and having a family.

"Look yo, everybody ain't meant to be all locked down with a wife, kids, big house with the picket fence and the two car garage. I like my shit just the way it is. When a bitch gets out of line, on to the next one. These hoes are just scandalous gold diggers looking for a nigga to sponsor them. Outside of a meal and a movie, they can't get shit from me. That settling down shit might have worked out for you but that shit is definitely for the birds when it comes to me and how I like to do things."

Markel shook his head. I could tell he didn't agree with me but hey, that was his business. "You keep thinking and acting the way you're acting and that's all you're going to keep coming across are a bunch of gold diggers and hoodrat smut-jawns. You're not going to meet your wife in the club, dawg. That's all I'm saying. The reason you attract those kinda chicks is because of the places you're meeting them."

"Alright yo, everybody ain't meant to be like you and Tierra with y'all little fairytale life. I'm not looking for a wife so it's all good. So just drop it, alright?" Markel nodded his head and turned his sound system up extra loud. Rick Ross was blasting through the system. I guess Markel felt so free to tell me what kind of woman I should get with and how I should settle down because he thought his little precious Tierra is perfect. I laughed to myself. If only he knew...

It all started our sophomore year of college at Widener University. It's funny how we all came up together. From John Wannamaker to Engineering and

24

Science, and then Widener University. Markel and I had always been tight ever since elementary school. We vowed to not only be best friends, but brothers also when my older brother got killed on 20th and Susquehanna during a drive by shooting. Nothing was ever supposed to come between us; niggas, money and especially bitches. It seemed like a lot of that changed when Tierra came into play our eighth grade year of junior high school. I'm not going to front, shorty was the shit when she started at the school. She had the body of a grown woman at thirteen with those big-ass titties and that fat ass. I guess it's true when they say women from down south are built better because baby girl's body was like that. I was going to holla at her. Markel knew I was feeling shorty. But he tried some ole slick shit when she was in the principal's office after getting into a fight in the lunchroom and got her number. I didn't trip though, and I definitely wasn't going to beef with him over no bitch. So I didn't say shit, I just let them do their thing. I thought it was just going to be one of those school relationships that only lasted a couple of weeks, maybe a few months at best. But they were like fucking Will Smith and Jada Pinkett. She was at all of his basketball games. They hung out on the weekends watching sports and playing video games. We got to high school and they were still together! The crazy shit was, the nigga hadn't hit it yet. She wasn't giving up no pussy, no head; NOTHING! She claimed she was a virgin and wasn't ready yet, but I wasn't buying that shit. Not with a body like that. That's what all smut-ass hoes say. Quiet chicks are the nastiest, sneakiest and freakiest little bitches in all of the continental U-S of muthafuckin' A! Markel was doing her mad dirty, though. Fucking bitches behind her back. He never fucked bitches from the same school, he always fucked bitches from other high schools. He had old jawns giving him money and rides to school and picking him up but lying to her saying they were his cousins or aunts. That shit was crazy because she never said shit. Either she was dumb as hell and didn't know, or she knew but played her fucking part. He finally hit our junior year of high school and for a while he had stopped cheating on her. I mean that nigga really tried to be faithful to her, especially when she got pregnant. But when we got to college and he saw how more experienced them college bitches were and how easy it was to fuck them white jawns, my man turned into a straight up hoe on the low. Tierra started figuring shit out when we were in our second year of college. Prank calls, silly emails, chicks writing love letters to him but leaving them in her door. She came crying to me one day but never said what exactly the problem was. She just kept saying she was tired. At the time I thought she was tired from the baby and trying to keep up with school, but naw, she was tired of that nigga doing her dirty. So I talked to her; tried to make her feel better about herself, gave her the usual cap up that niggas give when a hoe is feeling down. I admit, the conversations we were having and text messages that we would send each other had me feeling her all over again like back in eighth grade. One night, I swung by their little apartment when I knew Markel was with one of his little honey dips, and I beat that pussy up. I knocked that shit out real good and gave it to her just the way she wanted it knowing that if I did it right, I could hit it again and I did. The whole spring semester I waxed that ass. I almost convinced her to leave Markel for me. But she started giving me sob-ass stories about how much she loved him and how they had a family together.

27

"So you're saying you don't love me? I'm the one who's been here with you all this time while that nigga is out doing him with any other bitch he can get. I've been here for you. I've been more of a family to you and Tamia than him, so what do you mean?" I said to her one night after we had finished making love.

"I wish you would stop saying that. Markel is not cheating on me. He has never cheated on me and would never cheat on me. And I know you've been there. And I appreciate that, I really do. But I can't just leave Markel for you. How would that look, me leaving him for his best friend?" She looked at me for a second and then turned her back to me.

"Were you thinking about how it looked when you were fucking his best friend? So you're saying you can fuck his best friend behind his back but you can't be with me in his face. What the fuck type shit is that?" I snapped. I couldn't believe she tried to hit me with that lame-ass rationalization. Was she serious?

She whirled around with fire in her eyes and hit the shit out of me. Twice! She went to swing again and I grabbed her ass and slammed her into the bed. I pinned her down and screamed in her face. "Hoe, have you lost

28

your muthafuckin' mind? Don't you ever put your fucking hands on me bitch, don't you know I will fuck you up in here?!"

She screamed back at me. "Get off me, Darnell! Your punk-ass really gonna hit a woman? Get the fuck off of me!" She struggled to free herself. I guess she thought she was going to hit me again. I don't make idle threats.

"If you're tough enough to swing on a man be prepared to get your ass smacked the fuck back."

We both stared at each other breathing like two wild animals about to battle in the jungle. She never looked sexier than she did at that moment; pissed off and ready to rumble. I pinned her arms above her head and kissed her hard and deep. I needed to remind her who Daddy was.

I turned her over on her side and put one leg up over my shoulder and slipped inside of her. She was still wet, slippery and sticky just the way I liked it. I thrust inside of her hard and deep and she moaned loudly and whispered my name.

"Don't get quiet now. Where's all that mouth now, huh?" I pushed her knee closer to her chest so I could go deeper. She cried out and started clawing the sheets.

"Yeah that's right. This Daddy Dick, right here. You don't disrespect Daddy Dick, do you?"

Tierra moaned and replied, "No. I'm sorry. Please don't stop."

I turned her over so she was lying flat on her stomach, legs straight with her back arched just a little bit so her ass was slightly up in the air and I slipped back inside of her. I put my hands underneath her to cuff her titties and gave her long hard strokes. The pillow muffled her screams but I could hear her begging me to make her cum again. I stroked her as deep as I could until I felt her explode all over my dick. Feeling all of her hot, creamy wetness excited me and I bust inside of her. We laid there sweaty, and breathing heavy with her body wrapped in mine. Her little freak-ass started tightening her pussy muscles around me. Women; no matter how much you knock it out the box, they just keep coming back for more. I rolled over next to her and pulled her close to me with my arms wrapped around her waist and my chin resting above her head. She locked her fingers into mine and with my free hand I stroked her long hair. Neither one of us said anything for a few moments. Nothing needed to be said. I knew I was wrong for what I was doing to my best friend. But evidently he didn't appreciate her with all of the dirt he was doing behind her back while she was taking care of their daughter, keeping their apartment together and making sure dinner was done when he got home, plus trying to keep up with college to get her degree. He didn't appreciate her strength or her beauty but I did. I loved this woman. And even though they had a kid together and she wanted to keep her family, I knew that she loved me too. I just needed her to do the right thing.

I kissed her ear. "Babe, you're still up?"

"Yeah, why?" she answered back in her afterglow voice.

"Look at me." She hesitated for a moment but then she turned and faced me but stared at my chest. "You know what we're doing is dead wrong, yo. Like, me and Mar been boys since way back when. That's my right hand man. He's like my brother. We've had each other's back through everything. I love him, yo. Blood couldn't make us any closer. But as much as you don't want to believe me, that nigga is doing you so dirty and you don't deserve that. You're too good for all of the shit that he's putting you through. You say he's not cheating on you but you're not stupid. You know. And I know you know what he's doing; what he's been doing. You're holding that nigga down, playing your part, taking care of y'all daughter, taking care of home and going to school, yo. You're beautiful, smart, and funny; you can get any man you want but you're putting up with shit you don't deserve to be going through." A few tears slid out of her eyes and I wiped them away with my thumb.

"You might not believe me, but I love you, Tee. I would never do you the way he's doing you. Trust and believe that, shorty. We can't keep doing this, though. We're either gonna have to tell him the truth or just stop all together. I don't want to lose you. But I don't want to keep playing this game either. I love you, yo."

That was the first time that I ever said fuck it and put myself, my heart, everything on the line for a female. She closed her eyes and let the tears fall. I wiped them away and kissed her. She pulled back and finally looked at me for a space of heartbeats.

"I can't." she whispered. "I can't leave him. And I can't tell him. I'm sorry, Darnell. I'm so sorry. But I can't."

My heart dropped into the pit of my stomach and shattered. But I wasn't going to give up. I loved this woman. And had Markel not pulled that slick shit to get her phone number, me and her would probably be together instead of us sneaking around behind his back.

I slid from under the covers and started to get dressed. Fuck it, I could shower at my dorm. I left without saying goodbye and she didn't try to stop me.

About a month and a half later she found out she was pregnant. I thought that would have made her leave Markel because I was positive that baby was mine. To this day, whenever I look at Tianna, I feel a connection to her. She reminds me so much of myself. She just looks identical to Tierra. She insisted the baby was not mine and broke it off with me. She changed her cell number and told Markel the reason being was because of too many solicitations from telemarketers. Next thing I know, four months into the pregnancy, they were getting married. That's when I was pretty much done with the both of them. Those two frauding-ass bitches deserved each other. Ever since then, me and Markel's friendship hasn't been the same, and to this day he still has no clue why. He just thinks it's because he settled down and I still choose to chase. So many times I wanted to put a bug in his ear but I ain't no snitch. So I said fuck it. No sense in me being stuck with a kid I wasn't ready for and even if I did snitch, what would I have gained? They would've broken up, me and Mar wouldn't be friends and she still wouldn't be with me. So yeah, fuck it. Ten years later and still no one is the wiser. But like the saying goes, what's done in the dark always comes to the light. And this bitch might think everything is gravy now, but sooner or later I will be there when the shit hits the fan and her perfect little world crumbles before her very eyes. I'll never chase another bitch again. I'm only after my paper. You can't trust these hoes. They are more scandalous and devious than the niggas.

4

Markel

Darnell gets so defensive whenever I bring up the subject of him possibly settling down and chilling with all of his sticking and moving and club hopping. My bad, I just thought maybe we were too old for that shit now. But I guess that's just how it is sometimes when you grow up with people. Sometimes, niggas don't want to grow up. They want to run the streets for as long as possible. I guess he can since he has no kids, no real responsibilities outside of his rent and other bills. Sometimes I get the feeling that he thinks I sold out when I married Tierra, like I broke some kind of Pimp Oath. I made the best decision for us. Besides, she's a good woman and it would've only been a matter of time before I lost her for good with all of the dirt that I was doing.

Shit, Mondays are the absolute worst, especially when clients are coming in and touring the facility, looking to invest and expand our business. New patients were coming in and on top of that, I am finally getting the assistant that I need. The only problem with that is training him. Today is just going to be too busy to be bothered with someone who is too slow to keep up. So for the sake of this mofo's job and the reputation of this facility, this Negro better have his shit on point.

I must say, all things considered, I have managed to become very successful. We have a very large facility in the greater North-east section of Philadelphia just outside of Bensalem. I am the leading Physical Therapist with four physicians, seven medical assistants, a few secretaries and finally today, my own personal assistant. We get so busy not only in this facility, but in our sister office over in Langhorne, not to mention the patients who we do home visits with, that I need someone especially set aside to handle my agenda for the week, meetings with new patients as well as lunches and dinners with athletes and their agents trying to wheel and deal to squeeze their clients into my time frame. I am a very busy man.

There are quite a few women who work in the office who don't seem to give a shit about the wedding band on my finger. I have a large picture of my wife in a frame on my wall and all kinds of pictures of my kids, family portraits, and everything. Hell, I even brag about my wife's catering business and framed the article of her when she was featured in the New York Times after her catering company was hired to do the food for the new Mayor's dinner party. And yet these femmes still try their luck. It's so funny how quiet they get when she comes to the office to visit me and their jealousies show. My baby is the shit and none of these pitiful chicks are on her level. Because of her and with the help of my family, not only did I make it through undergrad, but I was able to obtain my Master's degree as well. She's been there for me every step of the way. Darnell on the other hand, seems more like he is just here for the ride. I try not to think that way about him because he's my home-boy. But sometimes, I just don't know about him.

My thoughts were interrupted when a knock came at the door. "Come in." I was engrossed in my paper work when it dawned on me I was hearing a woman's voice saying her name was Candice and she was my new assistant. I looked up at her with a perplex expression.

"Are you sure?" I asked as I pulled a folder from my desk and flipped it open. "I was expecting a Stephen

Carlson." I wanted to say that I was expecting a man, but I didn't want to be rude.

"Yes, I understand, sir. There was a last minute change where I was sent instead of Stephen. He accepted another position."

I looked Candice over managing to keep a straight and professional expression on my face. She was a tall, gorgeous woman with long, blonde hair. Her eyes were as grey as a storm ridden sky and she had high cheek bones with pouty lips. I detected an accent; English, perhaps, something European. Just from the quick once over that I gave her, I could tell she had a nice body; slim waist, slender hips, legs that went on for days hidden by her elegant gray business skirt and matching vest with black buttons adorning the front. Her jewelry was moderate, not too flashy, with a pair of dangling diamond earrings to polish off her look: Classy. If I weren't married, I would…

"Mr. Davis?" I heard Candice's voice interrupting my thoughts, which were trailing off to a very perverse place.

"Yes, I'm just a little caught off guard since I was expecting someone else, but nevertheless, you're here. You can have a seat."

Candice smoothed her skirt down and gracefully took a seat. She reached in her black leather brief case and pulled out a manila folder that contained her resume, cover letter and references. "Though the agency had confidence that I would fill the position adequately and this was a last minute placement, I just wanted to give you the opportunity to look over my credentials and decide for yourself whether or not you want me to fill this position, Mr. Davis."

Home-girl was on point. I took her information with a smile. "That's not a problem at all. Very professional, I appreciate that. Please, call me Markel," I replied with a charming smile.

Candice blushed. I still had it. "With all due respect, Mr. Davis, I believe in professionalism while in the office and think it's best if I address you accordingly as my hopeful boss."

My smile widened as I nodded my head in agreement. "I definitely respect that." I looked over her resume and then looked up at her. "It says you were the personal assistant for Sean Combs for two years. How did that work out for you?"

"Well, Mr. Combs is very demanding, but I still managed to meet his standards of professionalism, proficiency, and tackled many tasks in a timely manner as he hates tardiness. And even with the demanding position, I still was able to main a 3.8 GPA and obtain my first Master's degree.

I nodded my head but kept a straight face. Though I was impressed, I wasn't about to show it that easily. "I see you are still in school at this time. Is this your second Master's degree?"

"Yes, sir. But that won't interfere with my work here, I can assure you," Candice replied with confidence.

"Well, things can get pretty hectic. I need someone that can stay on their toes and is constantly and consistently on point."

Candice smiled. I detected a hint of cockiness. "With all due respect Mr. Davis, I was P. Diddy's assistant for two years. I think I can handle anything that you throw my way and more."

"Yeah but I bet you wouldn't be able to handle this dick if I threw it your way." I chuckled at that thought which I could

tell by the look on her face, confused her. "Well, I guess that about sums it all up." I held out my hand to shake hers. "Welcome aboard." She shook my hand and I noticed she had a firm grip. "Let me give you a tour of the facility and introduce you to some of the other employees here." I stood up and opened the door for her. I couldn't help taking a peek at her ass when she walked past me. Hey, what can I say? I'm a man. White girls have nice asses, too. I reminded myself that I am happily married and my dog days are over. I walked her around the facility and began introducing her to her new co-workers. I saved Darnell for last, of course. I prayed that he maintained his professionalism and didn't try to crack on my new assistant. Sometimes you just didn't know with him…

5

Darnell

I was kicked back at my desk thinking about the little honey dip that I met before coming into work. I was already plotting and scheming on how I would get into those jeans when I noticed Markel walking around the office with a sweet piece of ass in a sexy business skirt and vest combo. I was curious as to who she was. Judging by the way Markel was introducing her to people, I could tell off the bat that she must be his new assistant. A female assistant though? That was something that was an unwritten rule with Tierra and Markel; no female personal assistants under any circumstances. I chuckled to myself becoming curious as to how he was going to explain this shit to Mrs. Perfect. They were headed my way so I sat up and pretended to be engrossed in some files that were on my desk. My phone rang before Markel got to me.

Yani

"Davis Physical Therapy & Associates, this is Darnell speaking. How can I help you today?" I answered in a deep, sexy, but professional voice.

"Hey Darnell, this is Tierra. Is Markel around? I tried calling his office but he isn't answering," Tierra said into the phone.

"Yeah he couldn't answer because he just met with his new personal assistant and is giving her a tour of the facility, introducing her to everyone." I made sure to let her know it was a female assistant. There was a momentary pause on her end.

"Her... as in she? His assistant is a female? I thought he was supposed to be getting a guy named Stephen? Never mind. Can you put him on the phone, please? It's an emergency."

"Sure," I replied as I flagged Markel over to me. He stopped at my desk and introduced me to his assistant. She had a sexy accent and I could tell she was digging me by the way she smiled and gave me a subtle once over.

"Who is it?" Markel asked me.

"It's Tierra. She says that it's important but if you want, I can take a message."

"No, I'll take it. Just one moment, Candice." He took the phone and I pretended to go back to my files though I was eaves dropping.

"Hey babe, what's going on? I'm a little busy right now," Markel said to Tierra.

"With your new assistant? I thought we agreed no female personal assistants?" Tierra said back to him.

"This really isn't a good time, Tierra. Did you want something?" Markel replied, trying to mask how quickly he had become annoyed.

"Whatever. I got a phone call from Tamia's dean. She got into a fight and is suspended. I need you to go pick her up."

"She got into a fight for what?!" I heard Markel bark. I turned my attention to him not even trying to hide my nosiness.

"Apparently it happened in the girl's bathroom and escalated out into the hallway. I don't know the details. I just know that she is suspended and has to come home. I'm out Delaware working on a contract for a catering job I'm being sought for so I can't make it. Can you please grab her?"

Yani

"Yes, sure babe. I'll go get her now. I swear I'ma break her ass up when I do," Markel replied as he shook his head.

"You and me both; tag team that ass," Tierra chuckled. Markel chuckled with her.

"Love you, baby." He passed me the phone and I hung it up.

"Is everything okay?" I asked.

"Tamia got into a fight in school and was suspended. I have to go pick her up." He turned his attention to his personal assistant. "Well, this is your chance to prove yourself. I have a family emergency and have to make a run. While I'm gone..." he whisked Candice away and started giving a rundown of what his agenda for the day was supposed to consist of and what he needed her to do. Since I'm basically his right hand man, Candice would be working directly under me. I couldn't help the evil grin that crept across my face. This should be fun...

6

Markel

Of all days for Tamia to pull some shit, she picks one of the busiest days at my job to do so. As much money as I pay for her and Tianna's tuition, she has the gall to get into a fight and get suspended. It's bad enough that she is one of the few black people in that school and is already stereotyped as being some heathen. But damn Tamia, don't prove them right. She better have a good got damn reason for letting some shit like this happen or I'ma rain on her ass like white on rice.

I pulled into the oversized parking lot of the Catholic school my two oldest children were attending. Every time I come to this place for some reason, the Bells of Notre Dame from that Disney movie plays in my head. Sometimes I look up to the tower on the top of the building to see if Quasimoto's ugly ass is looking down at me. It took a lot for me to suppress my laughter as I walked into the building and made my way over to the main office. I had to at least appear to be a concerned parent. How would I be viewed if I walked in cracking the fuck up over an imaginary Disney character? Yeah, fucking ridiculous...

"My name is Markel Davis. I am the parent of Tamia Davis. I was told I needed to come pick her up because she allegedly started a fight and is being suspended." I had to throw the word *allegedly* in there. Shit, White people are always innocent until proven guilty and can use that *allegedly* shit, so could my baby. Innocent until proven guilty. Yup!

The receptionist looked me over, scanning my freshly cut, wavy hair to my smooth light-brown skin, neatly trimmed goatee, my pressed Armani Collezioni dress shirt, and matching Armani Collezioni slacks. Her expression changed once the fragrance of my Burberry cologne invaded her nostrils. Her appearance became a little friendlier, but not by much.

"I would need to see some ID," she said in a stern voice.

I reached in my back pocket and pulled out my hunter green and chocolate brown Salvatore Ferragamo wallet and retrieved my driver's license. She plucked it from my fingers and looked it over glancing up at me to

47

be sure we were one in the same. This bitch really takes her job too seriously.

"One moment, please." She handed me back my license and then made a phone call to have Tamia sent down. "I need you to sign her out here," she said as she handed me a book. "And also, a parent-teacher conference will need to be scheduled upon her reinstatement so the rules can be reiterated in case she's forgotten them, and also to get to the bottom of this matter to make sure it doesn't happen again."

I looked at her for a space of heartbeats. I reminded myself to remain the mature and responsible father I am because this old bag was about to get a taste of North Philly that would have sent her quivering in a corner like a horror movie whore being chased naked through the woods by Jason himself. "She knows the rules and she will be dealt with accordingly. You have a good day."

I turned to go sit in the hallway while I waited for Tamia to come down the stairs. A minute or so later, she was walking over to me with her head high as if she had something to be proud of. She seriously needed to be knocked down a peg or two. The look I gave her said more than my mouth needed to because she quickly humbled herself, hunched her shoulders and then sulked out of the doors leading to the parking lot.

"You wanna tell me what the hell is going on, Tamia? What the hell are you doing fighting in school?!"

"Daddy, it wasn't even my fault! They tried to jump me in the bathroom like I was some nut!" Tamia piped.

I unlocked and opened her door for her to climb in and then got in on the other side after closing her door behind her. "What the hell do you mean they tried to jump you in the bathroom? What for? Did you tell the dean this?" I asked her as I started the car.

"Yes, I told Mr. Rutkowski when we were all in his office. But they all lied…" she caught the look I gave her and cleared her throat. "…I mean, they started telling stories, switching up what happened."

"Okay, so tell me what happened? And no lies Tamia, because I swear your attitude and your mouth lately are really about to get you a beat down." I let the car warm up as Tamia began telling me what happened.

"During homeroom, I went to the bathroom because it felt like something was sticking me in my bra and I wanted to fix it. So while I'm in the bathroom fixing myself, Brittany, Chelsea, and Sarah comes into the

49

bathroom behind me. I didn't really pay them any mind, I just went on with what I was doing. So then Brittany started talking all this smack about how I swear I'm cute but I wasn't nothing but a yellow wench, and the only reason the boys who hang around the building after school wanted to talk to me is because I stuff my bra," Tamia explained.

Did that cunt call my daughter a wench? Oh hell no. "And then what happened?"

"I said 'whatever' and tried to walk out of the bathroom but Brittany got in my way. I said 'excuse me' and tried to step around her but she kept stepping in my way. So I stood there looking at her and her little friends and then she says, 'I dare you to hit me, I'll beat the black off of you, B'."

I interrupted her. "She said 'B' or she actually called you a bitch?" I asked her.

"She said the actual word. So I dropped my bag and said, 'you a frog, nigga, leap'."

I burst out laughing not meaning to. My daughter is a straight up G! "My bad, I ain't mean to laugh. Then what happened?"

Yani

Tamia chuckled with me and continued on. "Then Chelsea said, 'who are you calling a nigger, wench?' and then pushed me into Brittany. Brittany pushed me back so I socked her and we started fighting. I grabbed her by her hair and started punching her in her face and her friends grabbed me and pushed me out the door. Brittany tripped over one of them and fell out of the bathroom too and I started hitting her some more. I grabbed her and threw her into the lockers and started beating her up. That's when Mr. Rutkowski came and broke it up and made us go to his office. He barely let me say anything and they kept saying that I started with Brittany and switched everything around saying I kept stepping in front of her and wouldn't let her get by but it was her. So I'm suspended for five days but they only get three." Tamia hunched her shoulders when she finished her story.

"Wait a minute, you're suspended for five days but they only got three? How the hell did they make that decision?"

"I dunno," Tamia hunched her shoulders again.

I tapped the steering wheel to my car before pulling out and making our way home. I shook my head at the modern day racism my daughter had to experience. Not only was she becoming a victim of the same jealousies her mother experienced when she was a teenager, but she was being treated differently because of her skin color.

"Are you mad at me, Daddy?" Tamia asked me, interrupting my thoughts.

"No… I'm disappointed that you were fighting, but I understand you weren't trying to start the fight, you were trying to prevent it and had no choice but to defend yourself. It's unfair that you were given five days and the other girls were only given three but after that ass whipping you gave little Ms. Brittany, I bet it will be a while before she tries to pop fly to you again," I explained to her.

"I wish I could go to public school. Then I wouldn't have to deal with those femmes," Tamia said with a frown on her face as she crossed her arms over her chest.

"It wouldn't be any different. Females are going to be jealous no matter what school you go to, what job you have, it doesn't matter. If you look better than them, dress better than them, are smarter than them and get more attention from guys, females are going to hate; it's in their DNA to do so unfortunately. Your mom went through the same thing when we were growing up." I replied.

"Yeah, but at least it wasn't from a bunch of White chicks who thought they were supposed to be better just because they're White. I get tired of having to work harder and take extra steps just to show I have just as much right to be in that school as they do. It's not fair," Tamia moped.

"Life isn't fair. Nothing is supposed to be easy and if it is, nine times outta ten, it's not good for you. Just because you go to a school where the kids look the same as you doesn't mean you will have it any easier. Hell, you could possibly have it worse being in a school with kids who don't come from two parent families, have no home training, are constantly trying to fight; smoking, drinking and starting trouble just because they don't know better and weren't taught better. And the quality of the education isn't as good. Don't downgrade yourself just to fit in." I had to school my daughter. I understood her pain but she was just going to have to suck it up. We rode the rest of the way home in silence. I knew my daughter was unhappy and I sympathized with her. But we're Davises and we don't punk out for nobody...

7

Tierra

I swear I'm going to hurt Tamia when I get home. Her attitude and her mouth are beginning to be a bit much and I'm tired of it. Markel is going to have to pitch in a little bit more when it comes to disciplining these kids. My career is just as important as his and I swear, sometimes I get the feeling that he would rather have me home 24/7, watching the kids, cooking, cleaning and running the kids to cheerleading practice, basketball practice and everything else. This is not the 1950s. He better recognize that and fast.

I was just invited to do a cooking segment on Rachel Ray's show and I want to make sure I'm on my A game. I had been playing around with some fancy Italian and Portuguese recipes and decided I would do a test run on them for a sampling I was doing with a hopeful client in a suburban area outside of Wilmington Delaware. If all went well with this sampling, I would be contracted starting at $12,000 to cater her gala that she was having.

That was almost as much as the job the Mayor of New York commissioned me for.

I decided for appetizers to try lightly fried chicken wing-dings coated with a sweetened Portuguese Piri-Piri sauce with oven baked Sweet Plantains; and lastly, to show my artistic nature behind my dishes, Portuguese Seviche Cucumber cups. I wanted to make some Portuguese Steamed Clams but I only cook with a specific white wine by Pompeian. I couldn't believe how many stores I had to go to before I finally lucked up on an old fashioned winery five miles outside of the city to get what I needed. I was placing my items on the counter when I noticed the attendant was giving me the stare down like he saw something he liked. I must say though, this man looked like he stepped straight out of a Zane novel with his mocha colored skin, bald head and eyes the color of burnt sienna. Just thinking of her many erotic novels that I would read late at night while Tamia was a baby with the descriptions of men who looked like him almost made me crack-up laughing. I bit my bottom lip to suppress my chuckle. I think he took that as my subtle way of flirting with him. He smiled at me and I suddenly felt warm and tingly inside. Stop it Tierra!

"How are you, today?" he asked me as he rung up my items.

"I'm doing pretty good today, and yourself?" I spoke back politely as I pulled my American Express Credit card from my Fendi wallet.

"I'm doing better now after seeing your beautiful face. Your eyes are stunning. What's your name? Are you married?"

I purposely used my left hand to flip my bang out of my eyes so he could see the 24 carat diamond ring and matching wedding band. "My name is Tierra and yes, I am actually."

He looked as if my response crushed his whole soul. "Your husband is a very lucky man. My name is Xavier."

"After 16 years, he better know it," I smiled. "Nice to meet you, Xavier."

He chuckled with me before handing me my bag, letting his hand brush against mine. "Pompeian white wine is mostly used for cooking. Are you making an anniversary dinner or something?" he asked me.

I shook my head as I adjusted the strap to my clutch handbag. "Actually no, I'm in town on business for my catering company. I'm about to prepare some dishes for a hopeful client and I love cooking with this brand."

"Hmm, sexy and can cook," he said as he grinned at me seductively while eyeing me from head to toe. Damn, it's getting hot in here. "I'm planning a surprise party for my mother soon and my siblings and I were looking for a caterer. Do you have a business card so we can look into utilizing your services? I'm all for supporting Black owned businesses especially when it's run by a stunning Black Sister like yourself."

No he was not using that lame excuse as a means to get my phone number. Ha... this boy thinks he has swag. I reached back in my wallet and pulled out a business card. As I handed it to him, he made sure he caressed my hand just a bit as he took it from me. It was something about the manner in which he touched me that sent sensations to places in my body that only my husband should have been sending sensations to. I casually rubbed my hand against my jacket while I adjusted my bags again to shake the feeling and gave a casual smile.

"Well, feel free to look into my services. I have a website you can check out and if you're interested, maybe we can schedule something," I said politely as I began backing away.

"I hope so," he said seductively as he continued to eye me. We said goodbye and I turned to leave. As I pushed open the door I couldn't help but to mumble out loud, "It should be a fucking law against looking that damn fine," I had to stomp my feet at the end of that comment. I hopped in my Range Rover and fanned myself before backing out of my parking spot and heading over to my client's place of residence.

8

Markel

I took Tamia to Chili's to get an early lunch and then took her home. Even though the fight wasn't entirely her fault, she still was on restriction for getting into trouble at school until after her suspension. I went back to the office and was not surprised to see that Darnell was in full creep mode with my new assistant, Candice. If he put as much effort into his work as he did into pulling chicks, I wouldn't mind promoting him to a better position. But as long as he didn't take his work seriously there was no reason for me to take him seriously. I watched as he leaned over top of Candice while she sat at a desk and could tell he more than likely was peeping down her blouse. I shook my head and made my way over to my office.

"Darnell, let me talk to you real quick," I said as I moved past them.

Yani

"Okay, gimme one second," Darnell said, barely glancing up at me.

"How's everything working out so far, Candice?" I asked my assistant.

"So far so good, Mr. Davis," she smiled at me. Something in her smile was absolutely sexy. I caught myself gazing at her longer than I meant to and quickly turned to head into my office. I shuffled some papers around and began gathering contracts and paperwork for a meeting I had in a few minutes when Darnell appeared in my doorway.

"Yo homie, is everything good with Tamia?" he asked.

I sighed as I glanced over one of the contracts I needed a new client to sign. "Yeah, she had some beef in school with some little chicken-heads. Same shit Tierra used to have to go through when she first came to J-Dub."

"Jealous bitches are the worst," Darnell sneered before chuckling.

"Yo, watch your mouth, we still got visitors in here not to mention my assistant," I said in a cool, stern manner as I looked through one of my drawers.

There was a brief moment of silence before Darnell responded. "You just cursed yourself, nigga…"

"Ay yo…" I said as I looked up at Darnell as if he were crazy. His lack of professionalism was mind boggling at times. "We're not on the streets. Yeah, I said "shit". But dropping the N-bomb and calling middle-school girls b's in the office when we have visitors is a whole different level. So yeah, watch your mouth." I shook my head at Darnell becoming annoyed. He didn't say anything in response, opting instead to change the subject.

"Richard Morris called in to push his meeting back to 2 o'clock. He said his flight was delayed so he won't get into Philly until after 1pm. Candice was able to shuffle some things around and penned him in for 2:15pm to give you time to meet with Jean Krisco for his initial appointment for therapy on his shoulder and back strain," Darnell said.

I nodded my head. "Okay, that shouldn't be a problem," I said at first. Then I remembered that Tianna had a basketball game at 3:15pm. "Damn."

"What's the problem?" Darnell asked.

"Tianna's game is today. I told her I would be there but ain't no way I'll make it down there in time. Tell Candice to come here," I said to Darnell. He called for Candice to come to the office. I looked up at him and shook my head. I could've done that myself.

Candice made her way to my office. "Yes, Mr. Davis."

"We have a meeting in fifteen minutes with a very important client and then we're meeting with Richard Morris before a therapy session with Jean Krisco. That's going to extend the afternoon longer than I anticipated. I need you to get my wife on the phone and let her know I can't make it to Tianna's game and will need her to pick her up..." I ran down some more instructions to her and then we both looked at my appointment book to see what else was on the agenda for the early evening. Pushing Richard Morris' appointment back was cutting it close. I still had three physical therapy sessions plus two new patients to work in. I wasn't going to get out of here until almost 8 o'clock. Damn, Mondays really are the busiest.

I happened to look up and caught Darnell eyeing Candice's ass. Some shit never changes. "Darnell, did you need something?" I asked in a subtle way to let him know to take his ass back to his desk and get some work done. He smirked at me and left the office. That's my home-boy and all, but when it came down to my place of business, he needed to get his shit together. I'll be damned if I get hit with a sexual harassment suit because he decided to make a pass at my new assistant.

After running things down to Candice, she quickly began making phone calls per my instruction. I noticed she saved my wife for last. That didn't go so well.

"Hello," Tierra answered.

"Yes, this is Candice Alexander from Mr. Davis' office. May I speak with Mrs. Davis?" she asked politely.

"This is she," Tierra replied.

"Hello, Mrs. Davis. I am Mr. Davis' new assistant. He needs you to pick up Tianna from her basketball game this afternoon as he will be in a meeting and will be unable to do so."

"I'm sorry, what is your name?" Tierra asked.

"It's Candice, ma'am."

"You don't have to call me ma'am, Mrs. Davis is fine or Tierra. Umm, where is my husband right now?"

"He's unavailable at the moment, would you like for me to take a message?"

Tierra grimaced, "I don't do messages. He understands that when I need to speak with him, he is to get on the phone."

"I apologize Mrs. Davis, but unfortunately he is on his way to a very important meeting with a client and is…"

Tierra cut her off, "Candice, that's your name, correct?"

"Yes, ma'am." Candice stammered.

"I don't care if he is on his way to the inquisition. Please put my husband on the phone, now. I do not want to leave a message and whoever he is on his way to meet can wait two minutes while he speaks with his wife."

Candice hesitated for a moment and then looked at me from her desk. "May I place you on a brief hold?"

"Not a problem," Tierra replied.

Candice placed her on hold and came over to my doorway. "Mr. Davis, your wife is on the line. She sounds a bit upset. I tried to explain to her that you were on your way to a meeting…"

I held my hand up to silence her. She was beginning to ramble like a scared lamb trying to explain to the wolf why he shouldn't eat her. "Send her call through."

"Yes sir, right away, Mr. Davis," she quickly went back to her desk.

"Mrs. Davis? I'm putting you through to his office, now."

"Thank you," Tierra said. Her call came through.

"Babe, I've gotta make this brief…"

"Markel, I am not one of your clients so don't talk to me like I'm one. Check your assistant and let her know when I say I need to speak with you, there is no if ands or buts about it. I am your wife and the mother of your children. No, I will not leave any messages; no, you cannot call me back. Check her and let her know," Tierra said to me. I could always tell when she was upset or annoyed because her southern accent became super thick and made her sound even sexier. But this wasn't the time. I had to stand my ground. I told my dick to heel.

"Tierra," I said with base in my voice. "I don't know why you're upset but whatever it is can wait until I get home so we can talk. But right now, I have to work. I already know you have an issue with my assistant being a female. But that will have to wait, too. Did you actually need something or are you taking center stage?"

Tierra was quiet for a moment which let me know I struck a nerve. "You know what Markel… the same way you have a client, I have one, too. The same way you have your career, I have one too and I can't just drop what I'm doing to play step n fetch."

"Wait a minute, hold the hell on, Tee. Step n fetch? What the hell kinda attitude is that to take when it comes to picking our kids up and making sure they get to and from where they have to go? This isn't I and me, this is us and we. Now the same way I can put my career on hold for a brief moment to pick OUR daughter up from school after she got into a fight is the same way you can adjust your schedule to make sure OUR other daughter is picked up as well. What the hell is the problem?" Tierra had a bug up her ass and she picked a bad time to pull this shit.

"I'll deal with you when you get home," Tierra said before hanging up on me. I took a deep breath and closed my eyes.

I don't understand Tierra. I make way more than enough to provide for my family. I make way more than enough where she doesn't have to work. Most women would love to be home with the children, taking care of home and not having to stress over getting to their 9-5. But Tierra is definitely not one of them. I understand a need for independence, but she doesn't have to be independent when I give her every single thing she wants and every single thing she needs. All I ask in return is that she takes care of my kids and home the way a wife and mother should. It's not fucking rocket science. Don't get me wrong, she's a great wife and an excellent mother, but she has this Chaka Khan "I'm every woman" attitude that's in the way like shit.

Darnell came back to my office and tapped on my door. "Yo Mar, is everything good?"

"Yeah. Same shit different toilet," I said in a low tone as I grabbed what I needed for my meeting.

"Hey, I don't have any afternoon appointments unless there's something more you need me to do. I can pick Tianna up from her game and take her home with Tamia if you want," Darnell offered.

I thought it over. "With what wheels though, my man? Your whip is in the shop."

"Let me use yours. I can pick Tianna up, take her to the house with Tamia and bring the car back to the office so you can take me to my crib tonight and go home," he suggested.

"You're right." I reached in my drawer for my car keys and tossed them to him. He caught them in midair. "Good looking out."

"I got'chu my ni…" He caught himself and cleared his throat. "Not a problem, boss," he said sarcastically. We chuckled together as he went back to his desk.

Darnell is a little suspect at times when it comes to work and his own personal life with the choices he makes, but when it comes down to it, that's my man, one hundred grand. Always got my back no matter what. Not a lotta niggas out here that still got their day one niggas standing strong with them.

9

Darnell

Markel tossed me the keys to his whip and it was on and popping. A black 2012 Acura MDX was made for pulling bitches. I jumped inside the ride and leaned the seat back some more. This nigga sits wayyyy too close to the steering wheel. I looked over the detail of this car for the first time while being on the driver side instead of being on the passenger side and admired the interior. Leather seats, in-dash GPS screen, Bluetooth connect to cell phones, voice recognitions, chrome covered gear shift and a banging sound system with sub woofers and speakers. Yeah, this whip was definitely made for pulling bitches. I cranked the sound system up and searched through the satellite radio stations until I found some Meek Mills. The base from the beat of the music caused the sub woofers to send vibrations through the seats.

"Hell yeah," I said to myself as I threw on my shades and peeled out of the parking lot.

Yani

I headed over to Tianna's school and sat in the bleachers to watch her play in the basketball game. I was tweeting some little honeys on Twitter and messing around on Instagram when I happened to tune into the game after hearing a lot of cheers. Little Mama had some serious ball handling skills. I watched as she played the point as well as shooting guard positions. She did a mean cross-over after dribbling the ball between her legs and then did a quick behind the back pass to a teammate who tossed up a lay-up. Tianna jumped up and down excitedly before throwing her fist in the air when it went in. I noticed I had done something similar at the same time. I tucked my phone in my pocket and tuned into the game, playing closer attention to Tianna.

She is the complete opposite of Tamia. That girl is more stuck up than Tierra was in school and needs to be knocked down a peg or two. I can see why chicks in school are trying to beat that ass. I hope for her sake she has rumble game like her mom. But Tianna is rugged and rough, just as pretty as Tamia if not prettier, but it's always been something about her that reminded me of myself. If I had a daughter, she would be like Tianna. I still wonder after all of these years if she's mine. But I ain't saying shit. Definitely not trying to take on a responsibility that I didn't ask for.

The game ended with Tianna's school winning by ten points. Her coach gave her a huge hug and some of the parents from both teams shook her hand and gave her high fives to congratulate her on playing a great game. I made my way over to where she was.

"Hey Uncle D!" Tianna exclaimed. She gave me a cool high-five. I looked her over and chuckled at how wild she looked. Her two French braids had partially loosened and I saw where she threw the ends in a ponytail.

"Hey Tee-Tee. Good game, Shorty. You showed out on the courts," I said to her.

"Yeah, she is awesome out there," her coach complimented before shaking my hand.

Tianna looked around. "My dad didn't come?"

"Nah, he was swamped with some meetings so I told him I would roll through, see how much game you really got and then take you home."

"Oh okay," she said as she shrugged her shoulders. She walked over to the bench to get her duffle bag and book bag. I looked down at her leg and saw what looked like a scar right below the side of her right knee.

Tianna grabbed her things and came back over to me. "I'm ready if you're ready."

"You don't wanna change? It's kinda cold out there." I asked.

"Nah, I'm hot after playing that game. I'll shower and change when I get in the house. No surprise Tamia wasn't here. She never comes to my games."

"She got into some trouble earlier and went home," I told Tianna as we started making our way to the door.

"That was her that got into that fight on the fourth floor earlier?" Tianna asked as she looked up at me.

"Yeah… you heard about it?"

"I heard it was a fight and that a White girl got beat up. But I didn't know Tamia was the one who beat her up. Nice to know she has rumble game. She's gonna need it," Tianna said as she climbed inside of the car.

I chuckled to myself. Great minds think alike. "You have a scar on the right side of your knee. You had a fall or something?" I asked casually.

Tianna looked at her leg. "Oh no, that's always been there. It's my birth mark. Kinda cool. Looks a little like a dollar sign. Maybe that means I'll be rich when I get older," Tianna replied with a chuckle.

I pulled out of the parking lot and started driving to Markel's house. "Yeah... maybe," I mumbled.

I made a pit stop at Coldstones and bought Tianna a celebratory ice-cream sundae for having such an awesome game. We sat eating it, talking and laughing. The more I listened to her voice, the more she sounded like me. Before I knew it, more than an hour had passed by. I quickly took her home.

Tamia answered the door and then threw her hand to her chest. "Oh my God! There you are," she said as she threw her arms around Tianna.

"Dang mom, chill," Tianna frowned with a chuckle as she hugged her mother back. "What's the matter?"

"I went to the school to get you from your game and you weren't there. I'm calling your father and it kept going to voicemail and I couldn't get him on the phone at the office. I was two seconds away from calling the cops."

"Ewww and put an Amber Alert out on me, Mom? You really gotta chill," Tianna said with a smile as she

74

dropped her duffle bag and book bag onto the foyer's floor.

"Don't play yourself, Tianna. You know it's nothing for me to pop you in your mouth," Tierra said sternly as she eyed her.

"Sorry, Ma." Tianna lowered her eyes.

Tierra turned to me. "I thought your car was in the shop."

"It is. But since Mar had a busy schedule and I was done the bulk of my work, I told him I would pick Tianna up from the game and bring her home. Lil' Mama got skills like crazy and they won so I bought her some ice-cream. We were so busy cracking jokes, I ain't realize that much time went by. That's why we're just getting here," I explained.

She stared at me suspiciously for a moment. I knew what she was thinking. But she had no worries. I wasn't trying to play daddy to anybody's kid. "Thank you," she said. "But it would have been nice if someone had let me know what the plan was instead of having me rush all the way from Delaware and then damn near go bat-shit crazy outta my mind when I couldn't find my child. If Markel would just get this girl a cell-phone…" she trailed off and shook her head. "Thank you," she said again.

"No problem," I replied. I couldn't help staring at her. After all these years, she was still bad as shit. Crazy body, still tight after three kids, titties still sitting right, ass still tight. As much as I wanted to hate this bitch for the shit she pulled in college, she still made my dick hard. "Is everything cool?" I asked casually, faking concern.

Tierra looked at me for a brief moment as she picked up Tianna's duffle bag so she could wash her basketball uniform. "Tee-Tee come get this book bag and get your homework done before you even think about jumping on that Xbox!" Tierra called upstairs. Tianna ran downstairs and grabbed her book bag and then quickly ran back upstairs. I still waited for her to answer my question.

"Yeah, everything is cool. Just some things me and Markel need to work out, no biggie."

"Oh, alright. Well I'm here if you need me."

Tierra looked at me and then quickly looked away. "Tell Markel to call me when you get back to the office."

I smiled knowing that was her way of telling me not to even think about it and to go on about my business.

Yani

Without saying anything, I left out and sat in the car a
moment before pulling off. I suspected she was watching
me from the foyer window. I smiled to myself before
starting the car and made my way back to the office.

10

Tierra

I was too annoyed to fix anything fancy for dinner. First
with that crap Markel pulled earlier and with him having
a female assistant, to Darnell being the one to bring
Tianna home. Something about him being around my
children, Tianna specifically, irks the shit outta me. He
used to suspect that he was her father and I told him he
wasn't. I thought he dropped it, but the way he looks at
her sometimes makes me wonder if he's going to start
putting shit in Markel's head. I don't know what for. We
will never be together and what happened between us
before was just me being young and dumb and looking
to get back at Markel for all the cheating he was doing.
Darnell is not relationship or father material. He doesn't
even have his own life in order, how the hell is he going
to look after a child? And for fuck's sakes, he lives in a
one bedroom apartment across the street from the
projects! Whatever thoughts he has about the possibility

78

of being Tianna's father, he needs to just let it go because he's not.

I opted for simplicity with dinner. Besides, obviously the skills I have for whipping up fancy meals aren't respected anyways so why waste the effort? Spaghetti with Garlic Bread and Sweet Potato Pie was on the menu for dinner. Boring-ass soul food. No big surprise my kids gobbled it up as if this were their last meal before walking the green mile to their execution.

I had a little talk with Tamia and decided not to be so hard on her considering she was going through the same thing I went through when I was in middle school and high-school. I gave her some tips on how to avoid the drama, also letting her know that beating Brittany's ass was going to send one of two messages- Fuck with me at your own risk because I will beat that ass, or other girls would try to test her as well. We both agreed that if females were going to be petty like this because she is pretty, smart and popular, she might as well go to public school. But after she told me what her father said when she made that suggestion to him, I agreed that he was right. No sense in being in a more hostile environment.

Obsessive Intimacies

It was almost 9 o'clock and Markel hadn't gotten home yet. I know sometimes Mondays are his busiest work days, but he's normally home by 8 o'clock, no later than 8:30. I poured myself a glass of Cabernet Sauvignon red wine. I turned the lights down and sat in front of the fire place listening to Maxwell's *Whenever, Where ever, Whatever* song. The sounds of the flames crackling against the wooden logs added to the way my music relaxed me. A faint sweet scent from the wooden logs burning teased my nose. I was tempted to call Markel to find out what was taking him so long but nah. We fought enough today and I wasn't about to turn into the nagging, clocking, bitchy wife.

I looked over new recipes I wanted to play around with when I saw the lights from his Acura pull into our driveway. I took a sip from my wine as I glanced at the clock. 9:18pm. Let's see what his excuse is.

He came in the house and I heard when he sat his keys on top of the marble top mantel. He came over and knelt next to me before giving me a soft kiss on the cheek.

I turned to kiss him on the mouth, "Hey babe."

"Hey," he said back.

"Long day?" I asked him as I turned back to the recipes I was looking over.

"Man, I haven't had a day like this since we first started the company three years ago. I'm beat," he replied.

"How's the new assistant working out?" I asked. I could feel his eyes on me. Yeah, I'm about to let his ass have it because he knows how I feel about female assistants. Those little bitches almost always try sexual ways to advance in a company or get in good with the boss. And the fact that he is young, Black and successful, not to mention handsome as hell, bitches were already lined up at the job waiting for something to go wrong in our marriage so they could slide in. So a female assistant was out of the damn question.

"I know what you're thinking, Tee. I was not expecting a female assistant. I was just as shocked as you are when she came into my office. I was expecting Stephen, not Candice."

"So, send her back to the agency and have them send you someone else," I suggested.

"An assistant that meets my criteria doesn't come a dime a dozen. So far she's doing a great job and I don't think it would be wise to just get rid of her only to end up with someone who can't do shit right and I have to fire them," he explained.

"And I don't think it would be wise for you to piss off your wife," I said as I licked my finger and thumbed through the pages of the recipes I was looking at.

Markel took a deep breath. "Tierra, don't start."

"Don't start what, Mar? We've talked about this."

"Yes we did and you know what, the shit is petty and it's sexist. How would you feel if a client didn't want to do business with you because you're a female?" he asked me.

"Oh, so now you're concerned about my work. Heh, that's funny," I sneered as I stood up and sat my drink on the top of the fire place.

"Wait a minute, Tee. What's that supposed to mean? I've done nothing but be supportive of you starting your catering company and showing interest in what you do. Don't try to pull that shit with me."

"Oh please, Markel. If you could have things your way, I would be a stay at home wife and mother, driving the kids from point A to point B, cleaning the house, having dinner ready when you get home and laying on my back at night."

Markel looked at me for a space of heartbeats. "We are not doing this tonight," he said as he made his way to the living room.

"Oh yes we are. Markel, you better not walk away from me while I'm talking to you," I said angrily as I followed behind him.

Markel turned around and looked me dead in my eye with a seriousness I had never seen in him before. "And you better check your tone when you're talking to me and lower your voice before you wake up my kids," he hissed.

I took a deep breath to calm down. "I don't understand, what is the problem with me wanting to work?"

"I make more than enough where you don't need to work, Tee. I give you everything you've always wanted, everything you've always needed. Same thing with the kids. You don't have to work," Markel said to me.

"It's not a matter of having to work. This is what I love, why can't you just respect that?" I asked him as I placed a hand on my hip.

"What the hell are you talking about? I never said I didn't," he argued.

"No, but that's how you act."

"Do I not provide for this family? Do I not make sure you and the kids have everything y'all need and want?"

"That's not the point."

"Then what is it, Tee?"

I waited a moment before saying my next thought. "Men are always complaining about gold diggers and how too many women just want to spend a man's money without bringing anything to the table. And here you have a woman who is bringing something to the table and it's a problem."

"I'ma say this and then this conversation is over. Number one, don't put me in the category with these other niggas out here who talk that shit because I ain't them and to compare me to them is beyond disrespectful. Number two: I don't ask, want or need you to bring anything to the table. Your job is not to provide, that's my job; to provide for you and the kids, to protect y'all and make sure we have stability because that's what a man is supposed to do," Markel said as he stood close to me.

"And what is a woman supposed to do? Cook, clean, fuck and have babies?" I asked back sarcastically.

Markel looked at me, frowned and shook his head. "If that's how you wanna put it, fine. At the end of the day, the only thing I really want you to do is handle the kids while I take care of business. That's how this partnership works the best. Anything else you do is extra. Maybe because you grew up in a house without a father and watched your mother do everything on her own, that's why you have that mentality."

I pushed Markel in his chest and shook my head at him. He went too fucking far with that comment. "I can't believe you just said that." I turned to walk away from him and he tried to grab my arm to stop me but I snatched away. "Your food is on the stove. Good night," I said. I snatched the stereo remote from the coffee table and turned the music off before I went upstairs to take a shower.

11

Markel

I know I hurt Tierra with my comment. I didn't mean for what I said to come out the way that it did. The comment on her father was below the belt.

When Tierra was eleven, her father was killed in Atlanta while coming from work. He had been having an affair with a female co-worker and her husband found out. The husband followed her father as he was coming home from work one night and shot him twice in an alley way. The gunshot wounds wouldn't have been life threatening had he made it to the hospital soon enough. But because he was left in the alley, he bled out and died two hours after being shot. The cops found him maybe fifteen minutes after he passed. If he'd been found thirty minutes sooner, he may have survived. What's always haunted Tierra about his murder is the thought of him being in that alleyway in the dark, in the cold, alone and possibly trying to call out for help but no one hearing him. I believe that it kills her inside because he was killed for doing to her mother the same thing I did to her for so many years.

Tierra's mother tried to take care of things on her own but because the insurance policy was barely enough to cover the funeral arrangements and Social Security gave her a hard time with getting benefits for Tierra because of the last name discrepancy, they lost their home when Tierra was thirteen which is what led to her coming to Philadelphia. I had no idea what Tierra had been through with that situation until she was pregnant with Tianna. When she finally told me that story, that's when I knew I could never cheat on her again. To put her through the same pain her mother endured was wrong beyond comprehension. It also made me wonder if she knew all along about my affairs but kept her mouth closed the same way her mother kept her mouth closed.

Knowing that my comment had hurt my wife caused me to lose my appetite. I went into the kitchen and saw that it was spotless. I couldn't help but to respect the fact that Tierra could go to work, come home, cook dinner, help the kids with their homework, have the kitchen cleaned and floors mopped, bathe the kids and have them in bed by the time I got home on late nights like tonight and still have the energy to entertain me, satisfy me and keep me happy. Those are the characteristics of an extraordinary woman. Not too many can do that.

I put my food away, shut off the lights and set the alarm before making my way upstairs. She was in the shower in our master bathroom. I closed and locked our bedroom door and got undressed so I could join her. I was expecting the bathroom door to be locked knowing that she was angry with me but was glad that it wasn't. I stood outside of the shower and watched her silhouette through its glass sliding door. She looked as though she was picking her nails. I took a deep breath and slid the shower door back so I could get in with her. I rubbed my fingers through her long, thick hair that was wet from the hot, steamy water after it had rained down on her.

"I'm sorry, babe. What I said was wrong, dead wrong. I didn't mean to hurt you and I'm sorry that I did. I don't wanna fight with you," I said to her softly as I rubbed her neck. She turned to me and laid her head on my shoulder. Though I couldn't hear her because of the melodious beats the water made against the shower floor as it rained down on both of us, I knew she was crying. I wondered at that moment how many nights had she cried while I was out doing her dirty? How many nights did she stand in the shower like this, letting the hot shower water rain down on her to comfort her while I was out cheating when I should have been home with my arms around her? How many nights did she lay in the bed crying herself to sleep as she watched history repeat itself? Those thoughts struck something in me that made me feel like shit. I wasn't there to put my arms around her back then when she probably needed me to, but I was here now and damn sure was going to make up for it now.

I washed her hair first, rubbing my fingers through her scalp to soothe and relax her before I began to lather her body up with soap and hand wash her. After three kids, her body was still flawless. Her stomach was still tight with only two tiny stretch marks that she had covered with a tribal tattoo which stood for "Motherhood". Her breasts were still firm and perky and her ass was as round and plump as the day I first made love to her. Tierra is a remarkable wife and mother and I wanted to honor her.

Obsessive Intimacies

I rubbed her Pink Grapefruit scented body wash from Bed Bath and Beyond in my hands until it transformed into white, soapy foam, and began rubbing her neck and over her shoulder blades. I washed over her back with my hands, massaging her from her shoulders down to the center of her back. Since she was sixteen years old and I saw her nude for the very first time, I memorized every line and every curve of her body. I studied what she liked and didn't like, what touch make her weak, wet, and submissive against my advances. My fingertips traced over the top of her ass cheeks before sliding down and squeezing them as if they were fresh fruit with sweet nectar inside made especially to quench my thirst. I kissed the underside of her ass cheeks before lapping the warm shower water from her skin. She placed her hands on the shower wall and arched her back. I stood up and lathered my hands with her body wash again, this time washing over her breasts, being sure to twirl her nipples gently between my fingers. I could hear her breath becoming exacerbated. I kissed her neck and let the tip of my tongue dance around the back of her ear before pulling her ear lobe in my mouth and sucking on it while my fingers moved between her thighs. I let my fingers dance between the folds of her smooth, hairless and fat pussy lips, rubbing her clit gently back and forth until my fingers were covered in her wetness. I put my finger in my mouth so I could taste her and sucked her sweetness off. I did it again, this time sliding my finger inside of her warm, tight, wet tunnel and then put it to her lips. She stuck out her tongue and licked up the side of my finger as if I were a Popsicle in ninety degree weather before slowly sliding it all the way in her mouth and sucking on it. She grabbed me by the back of my head and turned enough so she could kiss me, swirling her tongue around my mouth so I could taste her sweet pussy. I kissed her just a little longer before stopping.

"You forgive me, Tee," I asked her as I continued to stroke her kitten with my fingers.

She moaned against my mouth. "No," she said with a seductive grin.

I pushed my fingers deeper inside of her until she gasped. "You forgive me now?"

She sucked on my bottom lip. "No," she said again as she shook her head. I laughed and slapped her on the ass.

"Let me get cleaned up. I'll meet you in the bedroom in a few. You gon' learn tonight," I said imitating Kevin Hart. "You gon' learn about this long dick."

Tierra burst out laughing and grabbed her towel. She stepped out of the shower and went into our bedroom. I washed quickly and then made my way downstairs to the kitchen. I grabbed a bottle of Hershey's Chocolate Syrup and squirted half of the bottle inside of a glassed gravy bowl. I put it in the microwave and warmed it up before making my way back to the bedroom. Tierra had already dried her hair and was lying across the bed with only our satin sheets covering the bottom half of her body while she lay on her stomach. I climbed on the bed and kissed the side of her mouth.

"Still mad at me?" I asked her playfully as I pressed my hard-on against her backside.

"Yup," she replied with a grin.

She might be mad now. But she wasn't going to be in the next few minutes. I pulled the sheets off of her and dipped my finger inside of the warmed chocolate syrup to make sure it wasn't too hot before I poured a few drops on her toes and down the arch of her foot. She jumped. "What is that?" she asked trying to take a peek over her shoulders.

"Turn around and don't move or you're going to be mad at me for a week," I told her.

"Dick punishment? You don't have the heart," she giggled. Her toes wiggled as she felt my warm, wet tongue slide up the arch of her foot as I mopped the chocolate syrup up. I licked down to her big toe and slid it in my mouth letting the tip of my tongue dance around it. I then poured a line of the warmed chocolate syrup from the top of her ass-crack to the center of her back and licked it up slowly. She moaned softly and laid her head on the pillow. I pulled her up to her knees putting her in the doggy-style position and began French kissing her pussy from the back. I stuck my finger in the chocolate syrup and rubbed it on her clit before sucking it off. I love the way she pushes her ass and pussy closer to my face. I lifted her up so I could ease my body underneath hers and made her sit on face. I licked up and down her slit until I felt her wetness drip into my mouth. I spread her ass cheeks apart letting my thumb press against her tight, pink, puckering ass-hole while my tongue spanked the hood of her clit, flickering from left to right, up and down and then sucking on it. She moaned loudly and sat up with her back arched and began riding my face. I buried my face in her pussy and ass and let my queen sit on my face as if I were her throne. I reached up to squeeze her tits and pinched her nipples knowing that would add to her excitement and like I wanted her to, she bust in my mouth. Most average chicks tap out after one nut, but not my wife. One is never enough.

I didn't even see her when she grabbed the glassed gravy bowl filled with the warmed chocolate syrup, but I felt it when she poured it over my throbbing dick. And just like she licked my finger, she slid her tongue up the shaft of my dick before swirling the tip of her tongue around my cum-hole. Pre-cum leaked out immediately. I squeezed her ass cheeks as I sucked on her clit, my tongue dancing around the hood mimicking the movements her tongue made over the head of my dick. She massaged my balls that were already tight with cum before slowly making my dick disappear down her throat, inch by inch.

Yani

"Oh, shit…" I groaned, my body shaking a little after feeling the slight vibration of her throat as my dick tickled her tonsils. Her warm, wet mouth slid up and down the shaft of my dick as she clenched her cheeks around it, letting her tongue press up against my shaft. Damn, her mouth was wet as fuck. I knew she was trying to make me cum but I wanted her to cum again first. She might get what she wanted though with the way her mouth was making the wet, slurping and slobbering noises that I love.

"Oh shit, Tee… damn babe," I groaned, coming up for air momentarily before nose diving back into her sloppy, wet pussy. And then she did it. She swallowed all 9 ½ inches of me but kept forcing the head of my dick to hit the back of her throat while she made her ass twerk on my face. I groaned loudly and started nutting. And oh fuck, she kept sucking as she caught all of my cum while swallowing and sucking. My wife is the shit!

"Who's the boss?" she asked in a dominant voice as she played with the head of my quivering dick with her tongue.

I was out of breath and dizzy as fuck after busting the mother of all cum loads. Got damn, this woman never disappoints. After I gained control of my muscles, I pushed her back in doggy style and got behind her. I ran my fingers through her hair and grabbed a handful of it, pulling her head back a little. "I am," I said in her ear. "Now, twerk on Daddy's dick."

"Make me," she said back in a defiant voice.

I gave her a semi hard slap on her right ass cheek loving the way it jiggled a little. She gasped and bit her bottom lip. "Twerk that ass, Tee." I spanked her other ass cheek and she arched her back and made her ass give my dick a round of applause. So my dick gave her ass-shaking performance a standing ovation. I rubbed the head over her sticky, wet pussy lips as she continued to clap her ass. I pushed the head in teasing her. She tried pushing her pussy back on me, wanting to feel all of me inside of her, but I pulled out.

"You're still mad at me?" I asked her again, gently pulling on her hair.

"No," she whimpered.

"You ain't mad because you want this Daddy Dick, don't you?" I asked her as I pushed the head in.

"Yes… please," she begged breathing deeply. I yanked on her hair and pushed my dick inside of her hard and deep making her cry out loudly.

"You better not wake my kids," I told her as I stroked her hard and deep.

She answered me but her words weren't audible as her face was already buried in the pillows to suppress her screams of pleasure. I could tell she was cursing, that much I knew. And I could tell she was about to cum again with the way she started bucking that ass back like a wild bull and tightening her pussy muscles around the shaft of my dick. I slapped that ass some more as I thrust my dick inside of her, fucking her hard and deep the way she liked it. I didn't want to end the night fucking, though. This was my wife and I loved her more than anything in this world next to my kids. I pulled out and turned her over on her back.

Tierra and I never have sex in the dark and no matter how freaky our love making session is, we always end it facing each other, whether she's on top of me, or I'm on top of her. And we always, always, look each other in the eyes.

I kissed her as I looked her in the eyes and entered her softly and deeply. Her finger tips danced over my back before squeezing me as she kissed me. Her body moved with mine and we danced to the beat of our own music, our moans sounding like an orgasmic chorus. But before she climaxed, her eyes became teary. She pulled me closer as we both climaxed and her body shook. But she was crying. That was definitely a first.

She shook her head as she struggled to catch her breath. "I love you…"

I was at a loss for words since that had never happened before. I didn't think it was a bad thing, but something about it was a little unnerving.

"I love you too, boo. What's wrong? Why are you crying?" I asked her as I wiped one of her tears away with my thumb.

She couldn't say anything. All she could do was shake her head as she continued to look me in the eyes. "Nothing… nothing is wrong."

I looked at her for a moment longer and then I got it. My wife fell in love with me all over again and it felt like it did the first time. I kissed her forehead and pulled her close to me, holding her tightly before falling asleep.

12

Darnell

I was able to convince Candice to give me her number after cracking a few jokes and throwing a few compliments her way. Hoes love to laugh and hoes love flattery. It would only be a matter of time before I would have her bent over somewhere waxing that ass.

Markel had just dropped me off and I ordered some Chinese take-out real quick, planning on watching the Heat destroy the Nuggets when a text message came through my phone from a number I hadn't saved. *"Hey Cutie",* the text message said. I wasn't sure who it was since I gave my number to four chicks today; the IHOP honey, Candice, a chick from the Chinese store and some other chick when I was on my way to Tianna's game who looked like she wanted to fuck me just off the strength of what car I was driving. I told Markel that car was made for pulling bitches.

I texted a random *"wassup"* back. Not even a minute later, the chick texted back, *"I bet you don't even know who this is"*. I chuckled as I chewed on some of my beef in garlic sauce.

"You're right," I said out loud. "And depending on how fast you jump on this dick, I probably won't care." Instead I sent a text saying, *"Why don't you just tell me?"* I cracked open a bottle of Smirnoff Ice and kicked my feet up on my coffee table as the game started. I was so into the game I didn't even notice that more than ten minutes had gone by and the chick didn't respond. Oh well, I guess she didn't want the D.

Just as the thought crossed my mind, a text message came through. I looked at the phone and saw it was the same number and it was Candice. I thought I put her number in my phone.

"Wassup sweetheart, wyd?" I texted back.

"Wyd- what does that mean?" she asked. I shook my damn head. Who in 2013 does not know what WYD means? I replied saying *"What You Doing=WYD."* She texted back saying *"Oh"* and went on to tell me that she was bored and didn't feel like going to bed. When a chick texts a guy after 10 o' clock at night to say she is bored

and doesn't want to go to bed, that almost always means she either wants to come over and get the dick or she wants you to bring the dick to her. My wheels are still in the shop and I'll be damned if I get on the bus to see a bitch. Plus, I saw that nice little Lexus coupe that she drove from the office. If she wanted this dick, she was going to come get it.

We texted each other back and forth flirting until after 11 o clock. The game wasn't as exciting as I thought it was going to be and I was tired of pussy footing around with Candice. So I told her to come through if she was still bored. I was expecting her to say no, but she asked for my address and when I gave it to her, she said she wasn't that far and would be there in twenty minutes. I jumped up from the couch and quickly began to straighten up. I didn't have a fly-ass house like Markel, but my shit was still alright. I had wall to wall carpet but there were a couple stains from beer and juice that spilled. I moved my coffee table a little to cover them and attempted to fluff the flattened sofa pillows. I put out some overdue trash and sprayed air freshener to get rid of the odor the trash left behind and then opened a couple windows to let some fresh air in. Then I showered quickly, and threw on a pair of ball shorts and a white beater. I was straightening up my bedroom when I heard my phone ring.

"Yo," I answered as I straightened up the dresser.

"Hey Darnell, it's Candice. I'm outside."

"Okay Shorty, I'll be out in a second." I hung up and grabbed the few clothes I had strewn about on my floor and kicked them into the closet. I then opened my bedroom windows and let some air in as well as turned on my ceiling fan so it wouldn't be so stuffy. I looked around and then went outside to meet Candice. She was leaning against her car with a long, grey peat coat on opened slightly and I could see she still had her work clothes on. It was something about the way the wind blew through her long blonde hair that made my dick hard and all I could think about was bending her over the arm of my couch and pumping my dick in and out of her tight cunt while I pulled on that blonde hair like a set of reins.

Candice smiled as she walked over to me. I showed her into my apartment and she had a seat. I offered her a drink but she declined claiming she didn't drink and drive.

Yani

I'm not one for beating around the bush and nobody goes to anyone's house at this time of night without the intention to fuck. I sat next to her and played with her hair a bit and asked, "So what's up?"

She glanced at my crotch quickly and then looked back at me while smiling, "You tell me." She was bold as fuck and I liked it. Not to mention her accent was sexy as hell, too. I ran my fingers through her hair and kissed her neck.

"Take that skirt off," I ordered her.

Candice giggled, "That was rather blunt."

"Listen, I'm not about beating around bushes. I'm a straight to the point type of dude, know what I mean? I know you ain't come over for coffee and croissants so are you going to take the skirt off or do I have to?"

She bit her bottom lip and stood up in front of me. I leaned back on my couch and watched her as she bent over in front of me after unzipping her skirt and letting it fall to her ankles. She was wearing a sexy pair of black French cut panties with a little lace at the bottoms where her vaguely tanned ass cheeks peeked out. My dick was already hard but that kicked it up a notch. Nothing is sexier than a bitch in pair of sexy panties.

"Take your shirt off too," I told her in the same tone.

She looked at me over her shoulders real seductive like and said, "No, not until you take something off."

I grinned, liking her style. I stood up behind her and pulled my shorts and my boxers down so she could see that big, black Mandingo dick I know a lot of White chicks crave. She licked her lips as if the site of it awakened a hunger inside of her and she wanted to devour me whole. I tucked my finger down the back of her panties and snatched her close to me making her gasp. She grabbed my hand and made me slide it down the front of her panties where I could feel just a small patch of hair above her little snatch, but the rest of her pussy was bald just the way I liked it. I rubbed my fingers over her pussy, getting her instantly wet. I used one hand to unbutton her blouse while my other hand played with her pussy and eased one of her small, perky tits out. She had large pink nipples that looked sexy as hell. I turned her to the side and rolled my tongue over her pink pearl before sucking it into my mouth. She moaned softly as her hand caressed the back of my head. I pressed my hard-on against her backside, grinding on her while I pushed her over to the side my sofa so I could bend her over it. I could tell she wanted that dick bad because she practically ripped her panties off and grabbed my throbbing dick wanting to do the honors of putting it inside of her.

"Ot'ine, baby. No glove, no love," I said to her, breathing heavy in her ear. No way was I fucking this bitch raw seeing how easy it was to fuck this bitch. I reached in the pockets of my ball shorts that were on the floor and pulled out a Durex extra sensitive condom and put it on. I put my hand in the small of her back and started to ease the head of my dick in, and got damn was her shit tight as a virgin! She tensed up and moaned as if she couldn't take it. Oh no, she was going to take this dick. I grabbed her hair as the head of my dick finally made its way inside her tight wetness and I closed my eyes not wanting to bust too fast. Damn, her shit was tight. I almost wished I didn't put the condom on. Warm, tight and wet pussy is grade A pussy. She moaned louder feeling the thickness of my dick invade her tight little pink cunt. I couldn't control myself once I was all the way inside of her and the way she moaned turned me on even more. She made the fatal mistake of talking dirty to me, telling me to fuck her like a slut. Oh yeah, ask and you shall receive. I placed both of my hands on her ass cheeks and spread them apart so I could see that tight, pink pussy swallow my dick as I pumped it in and out of her. I gave her long, hard thrusts making her moan louder and louder.

"Yeah, you like this big, Black, nigga dick, don't you?" I teased her as I fucked her deeper.

"Yes, I love that Black dick… mmm fuck me harder," she moaned back.

Even though her shit was tight and wet, it would have been better if she would've thrown that shit back. I hate lazy pussy. I grabbed her by her hips and fucked her harder until I could hear the slapping noise my hips made against her ass cheeks. It was beginning to sound like a freak-ass Dr. Dre beat between the noises I made against her ass cheeks and the moaning that she was doing. Even though I don't like to cum too quickly, she was just a late night booty call so it was no point in me holding back. I pumped harder and faster and the bitch squirted all over my dick. Oh shit! I love a bitch that can squirt! That shit drove me crazy and busted a knee-trembling nut. I grabbed her ass cheeks and jiggled them on my dick before pulling out. It was hot as fuck despite the windows being open.

I walked down the hall to the bathroom and dropped the condom in the toilet before flushing. I grabbed my washcloth and washed myself off before getting a fresh wash cloth and taking it back to Candice.

This chick was kicked back on my couch. I hope her ass don't think she's staying. I don't even play that shit.

"Here you go," I said to her as I handed her the wash cloth. She took it from me hesitantly as if she was confused. I began turning off the TV and moving things around to give her the hint to get her clothes back on and take her fucking ass home. She cleaned herself off and fixed her clothes attempting to make small conversation. I was hoping my short answers would get the point across.

"I need to check my work email before I head to bed. Hopefully tomorrow won't be as busy as today. I'm tired as shit," I said as I walked over to my front door. That was the last subtle hint I was going to give her before the ignorant Darnell in me came out and told her to get the fuck out.

"Yeah, today was busy, but it wasn't too bad. I'll see you tomorrow. Maybe we can have lunch," she said as she smiled at me. I smiled back but didn't respond. When I opened the door for her, she tried to kiss me but I leaned back.

"My bad, I'm not big on kissing," I lied. Actually, I don't kiss hoes on the mouth. No telling how much dick had been in there. She had the worst salty look on her face.

"Okay, I'll text you when I get in." I nodded and closed the door after she left out, not even looking to see if she made it to her car. She's a big girl.

Candice had a nice shot. And I wouldn't even mind tapping that on a regular while it's cold out. As long as she behaves herself and doesn't try any of that dating shit, she can get another taste of this Mandingo dick.

After turning off my lights and making sure everything was locked up, I went to my bedroom and got in the bed. For some reason, Tierra popped in my head. I thought back to how I used to bend her over and give it to her until her pussy juice dripped down my dick. I thought back to the way her ass jiggled as she threw that ass back. Her ass looked fucking amazing whenever I

108

poured coconut oil on it and shined it up and she would clap that ass on my dick. It was amazing how she could keep a steady rhythm while tightening her pussy muscles around my dick. Damn, that woman had some of the best pussy I ever had in my life and I had my share of good pussy. Reminiscing on that made my dick hard again and I started stroking it. It wasn't long before I blew another load thinking about Tierra's ass bouncing on my dick while I fucked her from behind. I'm wrong as shit for beating my dick to my man's wife but hey, at least I ain't fucking her no more. I chuckled to myself at that last thought before I wiped myself off with a t-shirt and then went to sleep.

13

Tierra

I woke up in the middle of the night in Markel's arms. To me, that is the safest place in the world. We've slept this way for more than ten years; with me lying on his chest with his right arm around me and with my hand on him. I looked up at him and listened to him breathe. It's amazing with all of the heartache he caused me, the only time I'm at peace is during moments like these; when we're lying together and everything is quiet and all I hear are the sounds of his heartbeat and him breathing. I never cried when we made love but my God, I am madly in love with this man. Nothing and no one can ever change that. I fell back to sleep and was surprised when I woke up after 9am.

"Oh no…" I squealed as I scrambled from the bed.

Markel appeared in the doorway with a tray in his hands only wearing a pair of pajamas bottoms. "What are you jumping up for?" he asked me.

Yani

"What do you mean? It's after 9am! It's after 9am and I'm just getting up. I haven't gotten the girls ready or J.R and..." I trailed off and looked at my husband seeing the devilish grin on his face. "Wait... why aren't you at work? Ain't today Tuesday?"

"Yes baby, today is Tuesday. But I already called my assistant and told her I would be late because I had an important meeting. Tianna and J.R are already at school. Tamia is in her room working on her homework for the week and I even made my baby some breakfast." He sat the tray on the night stand beside our bed and kissed me. "Good morning, baby."

I blushed and kissed him back. "Good morning. Aww, you fixed me breakfast in bed and got the kids ready this morning."

"Yeah, I know you get tired so like I told you before, I got your back. Tag team, boo. That's what we do." He ran his fingers through my hair and kissed my forehead. Like I said; I am so in love with this man.

"What did you fix me?" I asked with a huge grin.

"Strawberry topped French toast with a little cinnamon and some Turkey bacon," he told me as he removed the lid from the breakfast tray and sat it in front of me.

"Oh-kay, I see someone has been paying attention to me when I'm doing my thing in the kitchen," I giggled. It smelled delicious. There aren't a lot of men that can throw down in the kitchen. I sliced into the French toast and ate a piece. Mmm, yummy. "I thought you had an important meeting this morning. Shouldn't you be getting ready?" I asked as I ate more of the food.

"You were the meeting," Markel smiled at me and winked. I smiled also and continued eating. My phone rang and Markel passed it to me. I wiped my mouth in a napkin and he crawled next to me and started blowing in my ear like we were teenagers again. I suppressed a giggle as I answered my phone.

"Tierra Davis' phone," I said as I tilted my head while Markel licked and sucked on my neck. Oh God, he was getting me hot.

"Hi, this is Xavier from the winery out Delaware. You gave me a business card yesterday so I could check out your catering company…"

I froze as I listened to this man's voice on the phone. His voice was a little sexy, sounding more like a late night radio personality person instead of a man who worked in a winery.

"Hello…?" I heard him say into the phone. Markel was sliding the tip of his tongue in my ear and sucking on my earlobe. I pulled away from him and got up from the bed.

"Yes, Xavier. I remember you. How can I help you today?"

"Well, I checked out your website and was impressed with the plethora of dishes you had on display. I also did some research and saw that you're scheduled to appear on Rachel Ray's morning show and even did that big dinner for the Mayor in New York. It looks like your reputation is unprecedented. Sexy and talented, like I suspected."

I cleared my throat and glanced at my husband trying to remain professional. "Thank you. Are you calling to schedule an appointment?" Markel was hell bent on having my undivided attention and walked behind me. He put his hands around my waist and pulled me close to him so he could kiss on my neck some more. Nibbling on my earlobe and playing with my nipples had me stuttering like some idiot while I was trying to conduct business. He plays dirty.

"Yes, maybe we can schedule something for tomorrow afternoon. Will I be tasting samples or just going over menus?" Xavier asked.

My eyes fluttered when I felt Markel kissing down my stomach and felt his tongue lick over the top of my... Oh my Lord, he plays dirty.

I licked my lips, "Umm... you could either do that... look over the dishes that I have on my website or... you could... um... um... you could..." I looked down at my husband as he was kneeling before me with the tip of his tongue licking the top of my pussy.

"Mrs. Davis? Is this a bad time?" Xavier asked me.

"You better not hang up," Markel whispered as he eased me back to the bed. I sat back and let him spread my legs. Feeling his warm tongue in between my thighs almost made me squeal. I breathed deeply and licked my lips.

"No this isn't a bad time. I was just... I was just getting some THINGS..." Fuck, Markel was sucking on my clit with an evil grin on his face seeing that I was having a hard time being casual while I was talking on the phone. "I was just getting some things together. Um… Look through my website… If you have an idea of what dishes, appetizers, entrees and desserts that you would like to have for your gala and would like to do a taste testing, I require a deposit which is explained on the site. You can make your choices and send them to me via email along with your deposit via PayPal." I spoke quickly and bit down on my lip to suppress my moans. I closed my eyes and shook my head. Damn, Markel was such a freaky, evil man.

"Look at me," Markel said before putting his mouth back on me. The look in his eyes when he is doing his cunnilingus duties is so damn erotic.

"Okay, that's not a problem. I'll send over what's needed and then we can confirm our appointment later this afternoon," Xavier said to me.

"Okay. I look forward to doing business with you," I said to Xavier as I look down at my husband and placed my hand on the back of his head so I could grind my pussy on his mouth. I was about to explode all over his damn face. I hung my phone up and fell back onto my bed moaning super loudly. Markel grabbed a pillow and tossed it onto my face. I held it close to my face to suppress my screams as I came so fucking hard. That is what I love about my husband. Freaky and spontaneous. Before I had a chance to recover from that orgasm, I felt him slide inside of me. He moved the pillow and I watched the way his body moved as he stroked me slowly and deeply. I prayed Tamia had her earphones in like she always did while she was doing homework. Of all weeks to get suspended she picked a fine one to do so. It's not often I get to have day time sex with my husband. I moaned and muttered explicates on how many different ways I wanted my husband to fuck me and how much I was going to cum on him. We changed positions with me on top and I rode the shit out of him. It never fails that when I ride my husband, I make him moan out loud. We talked so dirty to each other. He grabbed onto my tits and squeezed them together before sucking on both of my nipples at the same time knowing that drives me crazy. Fuck it, I didn't care that Tamia was home. I put his dick in a choke hold by squeezing my pussy muscles around him and smiled at the faces he was making, easily seeing he was loving it. Then I grabbed a hold of both of my ass cheeks, spreading them apart and rode his ass like a porn star fucking for a check. I came so hard and moaned so loudly. Markel grabbed a hold of my hips as I held onto his arms and began thrusting upward, making me cum even harder. I could feel all of his hot stickiness shoot inside of me. I collapsed on top of him, both of us breathing heavy. He moved my hair out of my face and gave me a long, wet tongue kiss.

"That shit was fucking amazing," I said breathlessly before we both started laughing.

"Yeah, too bad I have to go to work or I'd tear that ass up again," Markel said as he grabbed my ass and kissed me again.

I rolled off of him and lay on my back looking up at the ceiling. Markel went to the bathroom to take his shower and I grabbed my phone to check my email. That's when I saw that Xavier was still on the phone. Holy shit… I never hung up! I looked at the phone screen wondering whether or not I should acknowledge that I knew he was on the phone or hang up. I put the phone to my ear and listened.

"Hello…" I said hesitantly.

"Well got damn Mrs. Davis," Xavier said before bursting into a wild laughter.

"Oh my God," I muttered.

"Oh my God indeed. Umph umph umph," he teased me.

"I don't know if I'm embarrassed that you heard me or disgusted that you kept listening to an obviously private moment..." I hissed in a whisper.

"Baby-girl, I knew something was going on with the way you were having a hard time forming your sentences." He laughed some more and I was at a loss for words. "I'll send that deposit right your way. I'm sure your food is very... delicious. See you tomorrow." Xavier disconnected the call before I could respond. I looked up at the ceiling and closed my eyes. "Fuck," I mumbled out loud. I was beyond embarrassed.

Markel got out of the shower and got dressed for work. I was wore the hell out from all of our extracurricular activities, so I was still lying in the bed. He leaned over top of me and kissed me.

"You need me to pick anything up before I come home?" he asked me.

I shook my head and smiled. "No. I'm going to get up soon and me and Tamia will have a girl's day out."

"Sounds like a plan," Markel said. He looked me in the eyes for a moment. "You wanna tell me what was up with last night?"

"What do you mean?" I asked, not sure what he was talking about.

Markel hesitated for a moment. "You cried during sex."

I looked away and bit my bottom lip. "It wasn't anything bad, Markel. And right now I can't explain it. But we'll talk soon," I said to him. He searched my face for a moment and then kissed me.

"I'll make reservations for you and Tamia to go to that spa that you like in Chestnut Hill. I want my girls to have a relaxing day, okay?" Markel said to me.

I smiled at him and nodded my head.

"And tonight, we'll have a dinner date at Chima. Just me and you. You think your mom will mind keeping the kids?" he asked me.

"I don't think it'll be a problem. You know she loves when they come over." We kissed again and then he stopped in Tamia's room to check on her before leaving out for work. My Nexus tablet went off letting me know I had an email. An order had been placed from my website by none other than Xavier. Apparently he wanted to sample my Chicken Jumbalaya, Gumbo and Dirty Rice with some Dumplings. The $200 deposit had been paid as well. I closed my eyes and leaned my head back into the pillows. "He better not try any slick shit..." I mumbled out loud.

14

Markel

I was expecting Darnell to be upset with me when I called him and told him I wouldn't be able to pick him up because of a last minute meeting. I knew he would be a little curious as to why he wasn't informed about the meeting and why he wasn't coming. Though this was just an excuse for me to have a morning with my wife, all of the business decisions that go on in my company don't have to be made privy to him. After all, it is MY company.

I got off the elevator and twirled my keys around my finger as I whistled a tune to myself. As usual, my employees came rushing over to bombard me with messages from clients who wanted to squeeze in a last minute session, phone calls from pharmaceutical companies who wanted to solicit their products and other calls. I listened to the chatter and then was immediately distracted when I saw Candice and Darnell at his desk looking a little too close for comfort. The sniggling and giggling as they talked closely let me know that their conversation was not work related.

I walked over to his desk. "Good morning, Darnell. Day two, Candice. Good morning," I spoke with a warm smile.

"What's up?" Darnell spoke, barely looking up at me.

He didn't catch on to the silence that followed his lack of professionalism in the office but Candice did. Her smile quickly dissipated and she stood up, clearing her throat.

"Good morning, sir. I was able to re-arrange your afternoon and early evening schedule so that everything fit in before 6pm. But I had to reschedule your meeting with Antoine Andrews, his agent called in. Apparently he had some legal issues to straighten out," Candice explained as she handed me a few organized files.

I looked over a few documents and then grabbed the one that I wanted after chuckling. "What else is new? He always has some kind of legal issue. Candice and Darnell, you two are with me today."

Yani

Darnell stood up and came over to me. "Um... I meant to tell you earlier that I need to leave a little early today. I have an appointment that I can't miss."

Not wanting to embarrass Darnell in front of Candice, I had to hold my tongue against what I really wanted to say. "What kind of appointment?" I asked instead as I glanced over a document.

Darnell hesitated for a moment. "It's personal."

"Will this be a sick day, vacation day or personal day that you're taking?" I asked him.

I could see out of the corner of my eye that he was giving me the screw face as if I had just asked him if I could fuck his mom in the ass. See, the problem that I've always had with Darnell is at least 3-5 days out of the month, he needs to leave early because he has some "personal" shit to handle. Ain't that many doctors' appointments in the world. Damn near one day a week, he's leaving early. But I'm supposed to pay him for a full 40 hour week? See how your friends try to get over on you? That's why you can't put everybody on when you make it. Niggas always trying to get over.

"I'm not taking a full day, just leaving a couple hours early," Darnell replied.

I shook my head and went over to my office so I could get my day started without responding to him. I had a great night and an even better morning with my wife and I wasn't about to let the dumb stuff ruin it.

I sat down at my desk and started going over my agenda for the rest of the week when it dawned on me what today's date was. Fuck, there was a business dinner that I had to go to. I completely forgot about it and Darnell was supposed to be my wing-man. The business dinner was with a couple of football players, their agents along with a couple of business associates from Nike who wanted to negotiate using our gym to film a commercial. Since Darnell had to leave early, he was just going to have to sit this one out. I grinned to myself as that last thought crossed my mind.

I picked up my phone and called over to Candice's desk. "Candice, come to my office for a second," I said to her. I scribbled some things down while I waited for her.

"Yes, Mr. Davis?" she asked as she appeared in my doorway.

"Looks like we have a dinner date tonight," I said as I looked up at her. She was dressed in another business skirt and vest combo, this time a black pin striped one. The vest accentuated her tiny waist and the skirt hugged her hips outlining her curvy frame. My eyes honed in on her tits quickly and I could automatically tell they were a B cup. I bet her nipples were large and sensitive...

"A dinner date?" Candice replied, snapping me out of my thoughts which were leading down a very perverse lane.

"It's a business date. A few members of a well-respected company along with some athletes and I are having dinner tonight to discuss a contract, and you are going to be my wing-man..." I hesitated as I smiled seductively at her. "Well... wing lady."

She blushed. Heh, the Dark Knight strikes again. I wonder if I'd made her panties wet...

"Will I need to change?" she asked me.

I looked her over and cocked my head from left to right as if I were trying to decide. "No, I think you'll be fine in that. However, I think I want to change." I reached in my desk and pulled out a slip from the dry cleaners not too far from the office. I had a sport's blazer and a couple of Polo dress shirts that I wanted to be picked up. I handed her the slip. "Bring those back with

125

a large coffee, no cream with two sugars. I had a long night, early morning and I need to be alert for this dinner tonight." I pretended to be engrossed in some files on my desk to keep from eyeing Candice. Her body was fucking crazy.

"Right away, sir." She left from my office and I looked up, taking a peek at her ass. I shook my head. I then thought of the dinner date that I had made with my wife and closed my eyes. Looks like I was going to have to reschedule with her. I picked up the phone and called her.

"Tierra Davis' phone," my wife answered after the second ring.

"Hey baby, are you still in bed?" I asked.

"Yeah," she chuckled. "You wore me out last night and this morning."

"I bet I did. At least you get to rest. I'm in here trying to pretend like I didn't just win a gold medal in the Hugh Hefner Fuckathon." We both laughed together. "Listen, babe. I completely forgot about a business dinner that I have tonight, so I'm going to have to reschedule our dinner date. I promise I'll make it up to you." Tierra was quiet on the line for a brief moment and

Yani

I could tell that she wasn't pleased with me cancelling our dinner plans. "I know you're mad but it's for an important client. Nike wants to use our gym to film a commercial with some NFL players. We're talking about a lot of money if things fall into place at this dinner," I explained.

"Sometimes it's not always about the money," Tierra sighed. I could hear the disappointment in her voice. It had been a while since the two of us were out together on a date without the kids and I knew she was looking forward to tonight. That was my bad for making the date with her without checking my schedule.

"I'm sorry, babe. I'll make it up to you, I promise."

She was still silent on the phone and I knew that was her way of not saying what was really on her mind to avoid an argument.

"I have to go. I have a client on the other line. Will this be another late night?" she asked me.

"Probably so if they want to visit the gym after dinner. So I should be home after nine again. I'll call when I'm on my way. Do you want me to bring you anything?"

"No. Good luck with your client." She clicked over to her other line and our call disconnected. Yeah, she was mad. I wouldn't be surprised if that wasn't a client, just her way of getting off the phone with me. I closed my eyes and hung up the phone. I needed to make time for my wife. Ever since I launched this company three years ago, it's been one meeting after another, more physical therapy sessions and at home sessions after another. No wonder she threw herself into her own catering company. She probably didn't want to be in the house alone all the time. My thoughts were interrupted by a tapping at my door. I looked up and saw Darnell standing there.

"I'm getting ready to roll," he said to me.

I glanced up at the clock and saw that it was barely noon. "Yo Darnell, this is like an every week thing with you."

"What are you talking about?" Darnell asked with the dumbest look on his face.

"This leaving in the middle of the work day like we don't have business to tend to or patients coming in."

"You're talking like I'm leaving before I finish my work. It's just paper work. And those are your patients.

It's not like any of them see me since all you have me doing in here is bullshit paperwork," Darnell snapped back.

"Bullshit paperwork? Ay yo Darnell, don't try to pull that card with me. You want more responsibility here, then act like it. How am I supposed to take you seriously and give more patients to you when you act like this is just a job and not a potential career you're interested in?" I said back to him. He was tripping.

"And what's up with me all of a sudden having to choose a personal day, sick day or vacation day because I'm leaving early? I never had to do that before." Darnell asked.

I looked at Darnell as if he were slow. "If your mechanic was charging you for eight hours of work but was only doing three, would you be asking me that question?"

"He's not charging me by the hour…" Darnell said back.

"That's not the point, D."

"Man whatever. I'm taking a sick day. I got something to handle. But don't worry, I'll be on time tomorrow and working a full day." Darnell left my office and I shook my head. He better be glad he's my right hand man or I would've fired his ass a long time ago.

I handled some patients for the rest of the afternoon, dealt with paperwork and hosted a conference call with our sister facility over in Langhorne, Pa. Candice returned with my dry cleaning and coffee and worked remarkably under pressure. She fixed my schedule very well because we were able to get our last patient out by 6:15pm and began preparing for our business dinner.

I was standing by my desk going over a proposal when Candice appeared next to me. I hadn't noticed that she was wearing flats earlier while doing all of the running around and taking care of business. She was now standing in a pair of four inch peep-toe pumps. Her long legs looked like they went on for days and the pumps heightened her curvy frame. I had a slight boner. *"Down boy,"* I thought to myself.

"I'm ready if you are," Candice said as she rubbed lotion on her hands. I snuck peeks at her as I put on my sports blazer and we headed over to the elevator.

This time of evening is when everybody is haul-assing out of the building to go home. We operated out of a ten story building and were on the 8th floor. The elevator wasn't too crowded but there were enough people on to forget about elbow room. I inched towards the middle of the elevator and Candice stood in front of me, slightly to my left. At the 7th floor, five more people decided to squeeze on. Candice took a step back, bumping into me.

"Sorry," she said, glancing back at me. She smiled when she realized it was me. I smiled back. She stepped back again and her ass pressed right up against my dick. I thought she was going to move but she didn't. She inched back a little more and I knew it wasn't by accident. I didn't move at first and if I weren't crazy I was positive I could feel her vaguely grinding her ass against me. I licked my lips and glanced from the left to the right to make sure we weren't being noticed. I gave her a brief bump on her ass with my dick to see if she would move but she pressed her ass back on me some more. Yeah, she was doing that shit on purpose. My dick was super hard and I pressed it against her so she could feel it.

By the 2nd floor we were on with only two other people who were standing in the front of the elevator chatting and not paying us any mind. Candice dropped one of the folders onto the floor. But when she bent over to pick it up, she pushed her ass all the way back onto me, bending over without bending her knees and picked up her papers, taking her time. This chick was really coming onto me in the elevator. I licked my lips again wanting to grab her by her hips and grind that ass up, but remembered my wife and stepped all the way back. My erection was raging and I could see myself doing some shit to her that would blow her damn mind.

We got to the 1st floor and left out as if nothing happened. She asked to ride with me to the restaurant with the excuse that she didn't want to get lost and risk being late. No problem with me. We drove in silence with the music cranked up as my way to distract me from our mini grind session in the elevator. I hadn't cheated on my wife in over ten years and though I had come across some women who made it very tempting to do so, I had been able to control myself up until this day. It was something about Candice that made me want to long stroke the fuck outta her.

Dinner went smoothly with lots of drinks and laughter. We were joined by my partners from our sister facility. The representatives of Nike were impressed with both Candice and I and were one step away from signing a contract with my company.

We went back to the facility so we could show them the gym. Impressed with our state of the art equipment and layout, the contract was signed. I was too excited! A multi-billion dollar company was going to be shooting a commercial in my facility. I couldn't wait to get home so I could share the news with my wife.

I was in my office printing some papers when Candice came in. She looked as excited as I was about the new contract we'd just acquired.

"You did pretty well at the dinner tonight, Candice. I was impressed that you knew so much about the company as well as the individual players who were with us. Not bad for your second day on the job. That was a big plus with them," I said to her.

"I thought it was because they simply couldn't resist your charms," she said in a teasing manner. She leaned on my desk next to me with her ass right above the edge.

"Sometimes being charming has to be included when trying to convince a major corporation like Nike to do business with you." Candice nodded her head as if she agreed with me. We began talking about how I started the company and what motivated me to expand on being a physical therapist, mostly dealing with sport's medicine. It had been a while since someone had taken particular interest in what motivated me to be so ambitious. Though Tierra always supported my work ethic and my dreams, she rarely asked questions about my business. I knew it wasn't because she didn't care, but showing interest sometimes wouldn't hurt.

Candice went on to tell me about herself as well; coming up in the UK with her father being a well-known and respected attorney over there. She spoke on how disappointed he was in her that she would not be following in his footsteps and becoming a lawyer as well. I stared at her while she talked and man, she was incredibly gorgeous. She looked like she should be more of a Sports Illustrated model instead of my personal assistant.

I hadn't noticed how close we were standing to each other until she licked her lips and looked from my eyes to my lips as if she wanted to suck on them. I caught myself looking at her pouty, pink lips as well and wondered what they tasted like. She was leaning closer to

me, close enough where I could feel her cool breath on
my face and smell the faint scent of the white wine she
had with her dinner. Before I knew it, she kissed me,
gently at first. She pulled back and looked me in my eyes
to see if I would stop her. When I didn't, she kissed me
again. I kissed her back, feeling her warm tongue slip in
and out of my mouth. I ran my fingers through her
blonde hair and kissed her deeper as she scooted back on
my desk. We slid papers and folders to the side as I
kissed over her neck. I could hear the clock ticking on
my wall along with her breathy moans as we unbuttoned
each other's shirt, and she pushed my sports blazer off of
me. I pushed her silky blouse back to expose her creamy
colored shoulders and kissed down the front of her neck
to her cleavage as she leaned her head back and rubbed
the back of my head. I unclipped her laced, white bra
exposing her large pink nipples. I knew they were large. I
sucked one and then the other as she undid the belt to
my slacks, unbuttoned and unzipped them and then slid
her hands down the back of my pants before squeezing
my ass. I found her mouth and kissed her again as my
hands slid up her skirt and found her matching laced
panties. My dick was throbbing hard and before I knew

it, I was putting it inside of her. Damn, she was tight and wet. That pussy fit my dick like a latex glove. I closed my eyes and bit my bottom lip as I grabbed her ass and thrust myself inside of her. She scratched my back as I thrust inside of her hard and deep. She was moaning too loudly so I kissed her again to muffle her moans. The pussy was too tight and too wet. I could feel her wetness practically raining down on my dick as she came all over me. Knowing I didn't have a condom on, I pulled out as I was about to bust and shot my load in my hand.

Her legs were wrapped around me and she was leaned back on my desk on her elbows breathing heavy. I grabbed some tissues and wiped my hand off and then squirt some hand sanitizer in my hands. I couldn't help looking at her small, perky tits as her chest heaved up and down while she struggled to catch her breath.

Suddenly I felt a world full of guilt wash over me. I couldn't believe I cheated on my wife again. I promised myself I would never do it again, I would never betray her or disrespect our wedding vowels. I felt like shit as I backed away from Candice and fixed my clothes. She fixed her clothes in silence and helped me straighten up my desk. We left without saying anything to each other and rode the elevator down to the lobby.

"See you at work tomorrow," she said quietly before walking to her car.

"Have a good night," I replied as I pulled out my keys. I walked over to my Acura and sat inside as I waited for it to warm up. 10:47pm is what the clock on the dash board read. "Fuck," I said out loud. I had no idea that much time had gone by. I put my hands to my face and shook my head. Flashes of the adulterous deed I had just committed floated through my mind. Worried that I smelled like sex, I reached in my glove compartment and grabbed my Izzey Miyake cologne. I dabbed a little on feeling even guiltier as I made efforts to cover my tracks and then called Tierra.

"Markel?" Tierra answered after the first ring.

"Yes baby, it's me. I'm so sorry. The dinner went later than I expected and then I had to show them around the gym and they wanted to do a test shot and run through. I'm on my way home now," I lied to my wife and felt horrible for doing so.

Tierra was silent as if she didn't believe me and she had a right not to. Finally she said, "Okay," and hung up.

I closed my eyes and sighed deeply before making my way home.

15

Tierra

This nigga must've either lost his fucking mind or he thinks I'm still the same dumb and naïve Tierra from high-school and college. I know muthafucking well that dinner did not extend till after 10 o'clock and THEN they wanted to see the facility this time of night for a damn run through. Seriously? Seriously Markel, you couldn't do any better than that? If that muthafucka starts cheating on me again, I swear to God I will fuck his world up. Not fuck his life up, fuck his world up.

I paced back and forth in our bedroom and stopped in front of our mirror. I figured I would make tonight sexy since we couldn't make it to dinner. Here I am looking stupid in this Victoria's Secret red, laced corset with garter belts, matching red thigh-highs and five inch heels; I've got champagne, chocolate covered strawberries, whipped-cream and hand-cuffs, and this ass-clown is probably out screwing someone else. I

stared at myself for a long time. For the life of me, I just
didn't understand what was wrong with me? How come
I wasn't enough and what was I lacking that made him
seek whatever the fuck he was seeking from other
women? I know I'm not ugly and I know I'm far from
bad in bed. So what the fuck was it? I shook my head
and swallowed back a glass of champagne. I dumped the
strawberries and whipped cream in the trash and took off
the damn Victoria's Secret and opted for a boring-ass t-
shirt. I was about to throw the champagne in the trash
also, but nah! This is too expensive to be meeting a
trashy demise. I poured myself another glass and drank it
back quickly before putting the bottle in our little mini
fridge. I turned out the light and climbed in the bed. He
better not even think about getting any tonight. I'm on
strike.

I heard Markel when he came in. I laid in bed
pretending to be asleep. I could hear him creeping about
in the bedroom, trying to make as little noise as possible
so he didn't wake me up. Then he made his way over to
the shower. I was beginning to feel silly and insecure for
automatically assuming that he was out cheating. Markel
had worked hard over the years to establish a good life

for us and provide for us and protect us the way a man should. He did some shit in the past but I could clearly see how hard he was working to make up for it. He still doesn't know that I knew all about the cheating he was doing in high-school and college. But he was dedicated to us now and marrying him means that I need to forgive him and stop being suspicious of him. That's only going to cause conflict.

I waited a moment before deciding to join him in the shower and make the best of what little time we had left for the night. Imagine my surprise when I twisted the door knob to our master bathroom only to see the shit was locked. Locked? Since when do we lock bathroom doors when it's almost routine for one of us to join the other in the shower? See... this is the bullshit that I'm talking about. You're locking doors now, huh? Okay.

I got back in the bed and waited for him to finish. It seemed like he was in there forever. This was a little bit too reminiscent of his cheating hay-days. Finally, the water stopped and a few minutes later, he came to bed. He eased under the covers and wrapped his arms around me, pulling me close to him before kissing my cheek and intertwining our fingers.

"I love you, babe," he whispered in my ear.

I closed my eyes and exhaled. "I love you too, Mar."

"I thought you were sleep," he said to me.

I shook my head. "I had nodded off for a moment but I woke back up." I pulled my shirt up, exposing my bare ass since I rarely ever sleep with panties on, and pushed back on him. There was a brief, awkward moment where he froze. I began to slow wind my ass and hips, grinding on him to let him know I wanted some action. He didn't move with me at first and I started to stop, thinking maybe he was exhausted from last night, this morning and then a late night at work but I felt his hands go up my shirt and he began to slowly twirl my nipples between his fingers. Yes! Thank you!

His hands moved between my thighs and began to rub against my pussy but it was something about the way he touched me that felt off. He lifted my left leg up and entered me, stroking me from the side as he continued to squeeze on my breasts.

Though I was enjoying it a bit, I wanted my husband to make love to me. There was something wild about the way he moved and thrust himself in and out of me. He then moved me in the doggy style position and

142

began fucking me hard deep. Don't get me wrong, I love rough sex with my husband, but something about this time felt cheap. The way he handled me made me feel cheap. He didn't talk to me like he normally did. I thought he was going to turn me over so we could make love as we normally do, facing each other. But when I felt the way he grabbed my hips and started ramming me, I knew that wasn't going to happen. And then he did something he hadn't done since the first time we had sex when I was 16. He came super-fast. What the fuck? No… this is not how we do things. He thrust himself inside of me one last time as he grunted. I guess he thought I was trembling because the sex was amazing when really I was disgusted beyond any form of comprehension.

I crawled away from him and jumped from the bed so I could run to the bathroom.

"Tierra," Markel called after me. I ignored him and slammed and locked the bathroom door. I turned the faucet water on so he couldn't hear my sobs. I don't know what or who that was but that was not my husband and that is not how we make love. Something happened with him tonight and I would bet money a late business dinner wasn't all he was doing.

Markel tapped on the door, "Tee, baby what's wrong?" he asked me. I shook my head not wanting to respond. I heard him twist the door knob. "Tee, open the door, babe. Talk to me."

"I'll be out in a minute." I put the toilet seat down and sat on the side of it, leaning my head against the sink as I cried. A woman knows when her man is cheating. I knew back then and I know now. But why? Why does he keep doing this to me? What is wrong with me? Just hearing those questions go through my mind made me sob even more. I put my hand over my mouth hoping that he couldn't hear me.

He tapped on the door again. "Tierra, can you open the door, please?" Markel asked.

I grabbed some tissues and wiped my face and my nose before splashing water on my face. I dried off with my wash cloth and looked at myself in the mirror. My mother went through this. My mother sat in our kitchen back in Atlanta crying so many times because my father was out screwing anything that would open their knees to him while she took care of home. I can't count how many times I would peep downstairs and hear her listening to the Temptations or The Dells and crying as she sat at our kitchen table because once again, Daddy hadn't come home. And the last night he didn't come home and she sat at the table crying, only for the doorbell to ring with the Police informing us that our father had been murdered, killed a part of me inside. I shook the memory from my mind and turned off the faucet water and turned off the bathroom light.

I unlocked the door and stepped out but Markel stopped me.

"Talk to me babe, what's the matter?" he asked me. I shook my head not wanting to speak to him as I tried walking past him. He grabbed my arm and searched my face in the dark. "Tierra, you were just in the bathroom for almost ten minutes crying. That's the second time you cried when we had sex. What is going on with you?" If looks could kill and he could fully see the way I was looking at him in the dark, he would have been a dead ass.

I stared at him trying to refrain from hitting the shit out of him. Instead I took a deep breath and said in a shaky voice. "I'm just tired."

"I don't believe you, Tee. Come on babe, you got me worried. Is it something I did? Are you mad at me for cancelling our dinner and coming home late?" he asked me.

I shook my head. "No," I mumbled. He stared at me for a little longer and then put his arms around me. At that moment I just felt numb and tired. I let him go and got back in the bed. A moment later, he joined me, wrapping his arms around me again. I shook my head as the tears fell. I wiped them away and prayed that sleep came quickly.

I woke up to Markel standing in front of the dresser as he got his things ready for work. I stretched and was getting ready to say good morning when his back grabbed my attention. I stared at what looked like scratches on his back. My heart raced and I looked down at my nails… which I wore short because long nails on a caterer just didn't seem professional to me. I looked from my nails to his back and stared at him for a long time. Long, red, nail scrapings stretched across his back, from the center going over the right side of his back and from the center going over the left side of his back. Not only did he lie, but he cheated and had the nerve to give that bitch the business with MY dick! A little voice in my head said, *"Keep Calm, Tierra. Hell hath no fury like a woman scorned without a pre-nup."* I took a deep breath and got out of the bed. In my mind's eye I saw myself walking over to him and smacking the bullshit out of him before grabbing the lamp and busting him upside his muthafucking head. But instead, I wrapped my arms around his chest and stood on my toes so I could kiss his cheek.

"Good morning, baby," I said as I looked at him through our mirror.

He grabbed my hand and kissed it. "Good morning, babe. Are you okay?" he asked me. Fraudulent bitch.

I smiled my beautiful smile and said, "Yes, I'm great." I grabbed some under clothes and a towel. I went in the bathroom and locked the door so I could get showered.

I was not going to cry, not to sound like Mary J. Blige, but I was not going to cry another time because he still insists on disrespecting me. I was not going to shed a fucking tear over the foolishness. I also was not going to let him get away with this shit again. I went so many years keeping quiet while he cheated and ran around with those bitches and yeah I did my payback dirt, but call me Karma, bitch. I make shit come back around after it goes around. And I never, EVER would have cheated on him had he not been cheating on me with those dingy bitches. I never would have disrespected him the way he has disrespected me for so long. I have been nothing but good to him during our marriage. I cook, I clean, and I keep the kids in line all while holding down a career. I nurture his ego; I fertilized his dreams and helped them to grow! I keep my body tight. I make sure I look good every fucking day even when I feel like I have one foot in the grave and I'm so exhausted I'm positive I'm sleeping with my eyes open. I give him everything and this is the fucking thanks I get! Men always claiming they want a good woman that can hold them down. A good woman that can cook, looks good, is smart, has good credit and can fuck. I'm all that and then some! And this is what the fuck I get in return? Nope, I'm not finna cry over his ass. I'm not finna shed one single tear again.

I washed and got out of the shower. The kids could eat when they got to school. Today is the day I'm not doing shit. I'm doing Tierra. I got dressed, fixed my hair in a fabulous style and grabbed my brief case with the contract inside for Xavier. The night before, I pre-cooked his samples and confirmed that we would meet at 1pm. But I was not going to sit in this house with Markel waiting until then. I didn't cook breakfast and didn't even put on as much as a pot of coffee.

Tianna came downstairs and looked around. "So umm… am I eating cereal for breakfast or nah?" she asked.

"Yup, milk's in the fridge," I kissed her on the cheek. "Fix a bowl for your little brother. Have a great day at school. I'll see you when I get home."

"I was joking mom… no red velvet pancakes… no buttered-caramel French toast…?" Tianna looked heart broken and I almost felt bad until I saw Markel coming into the kitchen. I snatched my keys from off of the table and grabbed my brief case before walking past him to leave without so much as saying have a good day or giving him a kiss. And that's something we never do. Whenever we part, we always give a kiss goodbye and tell each other to have a good day. But we also don't fuck in the dark. Since he wants to get all Obama on me with this change shit, I can too.

"Tee…" I heard Markel say as I walked over to the door. I didn't even look back as I slammed the door behind me when I left. Tianna looked at her father and he looked at her. He came out of the house as I was putting my seat belt on and tapped on my window. I started the car. "Tierra, what the hell is your problem?" he asked me when I wouldn't roll the window down.

I looked at him and threw my sunglasses on before backing out of our driveway and pulled off. It was barely 8 o'clock in the morning and not too many places for me to go. I thought of going to my mother's house and venting to her, but I knew what her response was going to be. My mother was a Nicheren Daishonin Buddhist and her answer to my problems whenever I tried talking to her was always, "The reason you're having the problems you're having is because you don't chant anymore." Sorry, but what did all that chanting get her during the times my father was doing the same thing to her that my husband is doing to me? That's like a Christian telling me all of my marital problems will go away if I just trust in the Lord, pray more and go to church. I wish people stop looking at religion like it's a magical cure for everything. It's not.

Yani

I drove over to Lemon Hill and sat outside just watching people as they moved about their day. My phone was going off back to back with Markel calling me and texting me, wanting to talk and work out whatever was going on with me. There was no point in me responding. If I came out and asked him if he cheated on me... no... not if... but WHY? Because those scratches on his back didn't come from me, I knew he would lie.

I couldn't help but wonder who the bitch was? Was it someone I knew? How long was it going on? And what did she have that I was lacking that made him flock to her? My phone went off again and I saw that it was Xavier.

"Tierra Davis' phone," I greeted, trying to mask my anger and put my personal shit to the side so I could take care of business.

"Good morning, Mrs. Davis. This is Xavier. I just wanted to confirm our afternoon meeting."

"Yes, at 1 o'clock," I said as I looked at my watch. It was already after eleven. I had no idea I had been out that long. I got up from the bench I was sitting on and made my way back to my truck.

"Great, I look forward to seeing you." We both hung up as I was getting inside of my Range Rover. I wasn't in the mood for the meeting with Xavier but whatever. I can't let personal issues interrupt my business because that interferes with my money. And for Markel's information, I don't work because I think I should, based off of some psychological shit stemming from my mother doing everything on her own after my father was killed. I do it so there will never be a fucking day that he can ever say to me that if it wasn't for him, I wouldn't have X, Y or Z. I've always been a go getter and will continue to be a go getter with or without him.

I made my way back to the house and packed up Xavier's dishes. Though I pre-cooked his food the night before, I didn't cook it completely because I like to lure my clients in with the aroma of my dishes, which is why I always have burner sets with me so I can finish preparing the food in front of them. Not only does it show my professionalism, but it shows my clients how thorough I am as well as my cleanliness. I checked the email for his address and put it in Google Maps so my phone could navigate for me.

I made my way over to Xavier's house and was shocked to see he had such a beautiful home. It looked like a family man's home. I imagined his wife would be joining him to taste test the food with him.

Xavier greeted me at the door and looked even more scrumptious than he did the day I first saw him. I could tell that he had just shaven because there was a faint scent of his after shave lingering that smelled manly. He was dressed casually in a pair of faded blue jeans and a plain white t-shirt. His arms were strong, muscular. Not like those body building ass-holes looking like Arnold Schwarzenegger from Conan, but fit like an athlete playing the Power Forward position in basketball. I suddenly felt tingly inside.

"Welcome, Mrs. Davis. Glad that you made it. And early, that's always a plus," he said with a charming smile. I smiled back as I shook his hand.

"Hello, Xavier. And please, call me Tierra. Mrs. Davis is just too formal."

He looked me over as if I were on the menu instead of what he requested before staring me in my eyes. Damn this man was fine. Even though Markel disrespected our vowels, I was not going to do the

153

same... regardless if this man looks like he just stepped out of Zane's *Sex Chronicles*. I opened my truck and began pulling out trays and he quickly came over to me.

"Let me get that for you," he offered as he began pulling the trays out and moving towards his front door. I followed him inside after passing him everything and locking up my truck. "This already looks delicious," Xavier said, taking a peek inside of the pans.

I smiled and began setting up the burners. There was an awkward silence between us so I cleared my throat. "So you're having a gala for your mother? Is it a birthday party or retirement celebration?"

"It's her birthday. She's turning 60 and we wanted to do something special for her," Xavier replied as he watched me intently. I noticed my hands were shaking a little as I completed my set up.

"Oh, my mother just turned 53 last month. My father would have been 60 this year," I said.

"Would have been?" Xavier asked with a raised eye brow.

I hesitated a moment and then went back to setting up the burners. "Yeah... he was killed when I was eleven years old."

154

"I'm sorry to hear that. My condolences to you and your family," Xavier said sorrowfully.

I shook my head. "It's okay… he had it coming to him." I regretted saying that and shook my head again. "Don't even ask… it's a long… crazy story."

Xavier nodded his head and leaned back on the counter continuing to watch me. God, he was making me nervous.

"Will your wife be joining us?" I asked as I glanced up at him.

Xavier smiled that charming smile which I am sure melted many of hearts in his day. "No, I'm not involved at the moment." He poured himself a cup of coffee. "Would you like a cup of coffee?"

"No thanks." After everything was set up, I began preparing the food and talking with him briefly about how everything would work out if he and his family decided to go with my company. He passed me a plate and I put a small portion of Jambalaya along with a dumpling on it for him.

"Mmm this looks and smells delicious. I don't doubt for one second that it tastes delicious." He put some on a fork and blew the steam from the morsel of food. The way his lips went together made my nipples hard. I didn't mean to but I bit down on my bottom lip as I watched him. He looked me dead in my eyes as he slowly slid the fork in his mouth to taste the food. The way he did it was so suggestive and erotic; I'm not lying when I say my panties became just a teeny bit moist. He closed his eyes as if the taste of my food brought him a little closer to heaven. "This is good... yes this is so good." I giggled as he hurriedly ate the rest of the Jambalaya and then went for the dumpling. He took a small bite and then licked his lips. "Yes, Tierra you are definitely hired," he said as he shook his head at me with a smile.

I smiled and turned the burners off. I knew he was going to hire me. I've never been turned down by a Black family or group who requested a sampling of my Soul Food. Call me cocky. I call it confidence.

"Do you ever taste your food?" Xavier asked me as he licked his lips again and eyed me.

"I mostly let my hopeful clients taste because their opinion is what's going to get me the job," I replied.

Xavier nodded slowly. "That's true. But I want you to taste this. I hate eating alone. Makes me feel greedy, you feel me?" I was going to refuse but he shook his head at me letting me know he wasn't going to take no for an answer. I was prepared to put a morsel of food on a plate until he walked close to me and picked up the dumpling between his fingers so he could feed it to me. I hesitated for a moment but went on and took a bite. As if I didn't already know, the dumpling was delicious. But it was something about the way he fed it to me that made it even tastier.

"Good, isn't it?" Xavier asked me in that damn Don Juan voice.

I nodded my head and licked my lips. "Yeah, it is." Xavier sat the plate on his counter and reached for my face. I jumped a little and he smiled. "Relax, you have a little right here," he said as he wiped the side of my mouth. I thought he would have wiped his hand on a napkin but instead he licked the same finger. "Yeah, I knew you'd taste good."

Fuck... now my panties are wet. I stared at him like some lost lamb in the woods wondering if the big bad wolf would eat me. He used his thumb to wipe the side of my mouth again and when he softly traced over my bottom lip, I opened my mouth and invited his thumb inside, suckling on it softly while I stared at him. He picked my right hand up and kissed the tips of my fingers before sucking on the middle one. Damn, his lips were soft and his tongue was warm and wet. I wanted to feel it in my mouth when he kissed me. I wanted to feel it in other places, too.

Xavier reached for the clip in my hair and removed it so my hair fell down to my shoulders and kissed me. I didn't resist him and I kissed him back. I thought of the betrayal Markel had committed and that caused me to kiss Xavier even deeper. He ran his fingers through my hair and pulled me closer to him. But then he stopped.

"We can't do this," he said to me as he breathed heavily against my mouth.

"Why not?" I whispered, flickering the tip of my tongue over his lips.

"You're married... don't you want me to stop?"

"Did I ask you to stop?" I asked in return as I unzipped his pants.

"Nuff said..." Xavier went for the zipper on the back of my skirt and undid it. He tugged on it a little as he tongue kissed me and it fell down to my ankles. This man picked me up while he kissed me and I wrapped my legs around his waist. He carried me over to the sofa and laid me down on it. He pulled my five inch heels off and tossed them to the floor before ripping my stockings off of me. Oh shit, this man likes it rough. And the way I was feeling right now, I wanted it rough. He put his face between my legs and began humming on my pussy through my panties. I arched my back and then looked down at him as he eased my panties down with his teeth. Yes, this is what I needed to help relieve my stress. Eat me, baby! Eat me like a starving man on a Philly Cheese steak! Eat me! And that's exactly what he did, but he did it way differently than Markel. Not only did he lick and suck on my clit the way I love, but he nibbled on it. Not too painfully, but it felt more like a pleasurable pain. I came so fucking hard but he just kept going. He didn't just lick and suck my clit afterwards; he slid his tongue in and out of my pussy as if he were French kissing it while his thumb twirled around the hood of my clit causing me to cum again. I don't know if I was more excited from the way he ate my pussy or if I was relieved that I didn't have to suppress my screams. I rubbed the back of his head as he continued to lick and suck on my cunt. I felt two of his fingers slide inside of me as he continued to suck on my clit. I began grinding my pussy all over his face causing him to moan just as loud as I did. After I came that last time, he stood up with his dick bouncing up and down. Damn, he was hung! And had a slight curve to it like a banana with a huge mushroom head that was already leaking pre-cum. I didn't protest when he began rubbing it against my sloppy, wet and juicy pussy. Instead, I raised my knees and spread my legs wider. I wanted to fill that dick in my stomach. The size of it and the way it was curved was a little painful at first and I squirmed until I felt comfortable with his endowed member inside of me. He squeezed on my breasts as he stroked me slowly and deeply as if he were teasing me. I reached down to my pussy and rubbed it a little, getting some of my sticky wetness onto my fingers and then sucked it off while I eyed him. He let out a groan and thrust his dick in me deeper and harder. I then squeezed my large 36 DD tits pushing them up so I could flicker my tongue across my dark nipple. I could tell that drove him crazy because he grabbed me under my ass and lift me up and started pounding my pussy. All I could do was scream, "Yes! Yes baby, give it to me! Yes, please fuck me! God, Yes!" I could feel him hitting my G-Spot which caused me to grab his ass so I could fuck him back. I came super fucking hard, squirting warm pussy juice all over his dick. I felt him tense up and I grabbed him tighter and pushed him in deeper until he exploded inside of me. He continued to stroke me slowly. I thought it was over, but he pulled out, got back between my legs and started eating my pussy again. Holy fuck, are you serious? What shocked me was how much that turned me on. He pulled me up so I could sit on his face and I face-fucked the shit out of him until I came again. My body shook profusely and I was sweating like crazy. That was the freakiest and most erotic shit I had ever experienced; getting my pussy eaten after having sex. Got-damn, that shit was good!

Afterwards, he showed me to the bathroom so I could shower and get dressed. He walked me to my car and gave me a big wet kiss.

"I hope I get to see you again, Tierra. Outside of the catering I want you to do for the party," Xavier said as I got inside of my Range Rover.

"You just might," I smiled at him. I threw my shades on and he watched me pull off. Like I said before: What's good for the Goose is good for the gander.

15

Markel

I think I'm caught. I think Tierra knows something happened last night. It couldn't be because I worked late because I always work late. No… she doesn't know. She's probably just upset that I cancelled our dinner plans. But damn, she didn't cook breakfast, didn't even make any coffee and didn't give me a kiss goodbye. And why the hell was she leaving so early? She rarely ever leaves early. Something is going on with her. Throwing temper tantrums, crying during and after sex, leaving and slamming doors. It's starting to make me wonder what she's doing…?

I called Darnell to see if he needed a ride to work but he said was cool, he'd already gotten his car out of the shop the day before. Oh, so that's why his ass wanted to leave early. I shook my head at how he tries to get over. I made my way into the office and saw Darnell busy at work. Maybe my words finally sank into his thick head and he would take business more seriously. I looked around for Candice and didn't see her so I went over to Darnell's desk.

"Hey Darnell, anything new this morning?"

Darnell was silent for a moment and then looked up from his computer screen. "You went to the dinner with Nike without me last night. And you took Candice in my place?" he looked at me with contempt. Here we go.

"Didn't you say you had to leave early for something personal you had to take care of? You took a sick day, didn't say exactly why you were leaving early so that left me under the assumption that you had some health appointment or something," I said to him casually.

"You know what happens when you assume," Darnell said as he shook his head.

"Oh and what should I have assumed?"

Darnell shook his head at me again and went back to his work. "You knew how much I wanted to go to that dinner."

"If you had said you needed some time off to go get your car out of the shop then I wouldn't have put Candice in your place. Don't try to put it off on me as if I did some sort of disservice to you. Try a little

163

professional courtesy and stuff like this won't happen."
Darnell better start remembering real soon that I am his
boss, he is not a partner and I had more than enough
reason to throw his ass to the unemployment line. Man,
he better be glad that he's my home-boy. But he was
really starting to piss me off.

"Fine, whatever," Darnell mumbled.

I was starting to walk away from his desk when it
dawned on me I still didn't know where Candice was.
"Where is Candice?"

Just as the question fell from my lips, I saw her
walking over to me hurriedly, her high-heels click-
clacking across the floors. She was wearing a high-waist
black business skirt with a sheer black and white striped
blouse. Her hair was swept neatly in a bun and she was
wearing eye glasses. The way she walked was as though
the office was the runway strip and she was owning it.
Damn, she had a mean ass walk. And I started getting
another boner.

"I'm here, sir. I apologize for my tardiness. I figured
I would grab your coffee, no cream, with two sugars
since I know you had a late night and an early morning,"

she said that with a slight grin, her accent adding extreme sex appeal to her words.

I couldn't help the grin that crept across my face as I knew what she was hinting at. But I forced the grin to quickly dissipate as I took the coffee from her. That was a one-time shot that I would try my damn hardest to insure it never happened again. "Thank you for the coffee, Candice and good morning. Are you ready for day three?" I asked her as we made our way over to my office.

"Absolutely," she replied. "Last night's dinner was amazing." We went into my office and I shut the door. Candice stood by it as if she were waiting for me to dish out the orders for the day. I stood with my back to her as I thought back to the sex we had in this very same room the night before. As good as it was and as sexy as she looked, I knew it could never happen again. I sipped the steaming cup of coffee and smiled at the irony. My wife didn't bother to fix me any coffee before leaving out this morning, but my mistress brought me a cup of coffee just the way I liked it without me even asking her. Ain't that some shit?

"Candice, about last night..." I started to say.

"Sir, pardon my interruption but I just want to say that in no way, shape, or form will I allow what happened between us to affect my position. And I am not one to sleep with my boss in hopes that it will gain me a higher position. I would like to blame it on the white wine I had with dinner, but that would be a cheap cop-out and last night was far from cheap…" she trailed off and fell silent.

I turned to face her and couldn't help but feel drawn to her beauty. I took a deep breath before I spoke. "It can never happen again. I am a married man. Happily married and I've never disrespected my wife in that fashion since we've been married. Hopefully this doesn't affect our work relationship as I am extremely impressed with how you have been able to handle yourself your first couple of days here. But last night can never happen again."

Candice looked at me for a moment and then nodded her head. "I understand, sir." She moved her jacket to her other arm and opened a folder she was carrying. "A few emails came in late last night and early this morning…"

Yani

We stood next to each other as I looked at the folder with her. The fragrance of her perfume teased my nostrils. I leaned in closer as if her scent were a drug that was alluring and erotic. She went over my appointments for the day as well as the few that were rescheduled, cancelled and then filled in by others who wanted last minute appointments. She glanced up at me and our eyes locked. It was something about her that was erotic and captivating. I couldn't put my finger on it but looking at her made me want to hike her skirt up, slide her panties to the side and have her sit on my di…

My thoughts were interrupted by my office phone ringing. Candice blinked rapidly as if she had been snapped out of a trance and I cleared my throat before stepping away from her so I could answer the phone. It was a business call, so I asked Candice for some privacy and she quickly left my office to take care of her duties. Another boner… I must be trying to set some record for number of hard-ons in a 48 hour time frame.

I tried calling Tierra numerous times and sent her multiple text messages but she refused to answer. My calls were actually starting to go straight to voicemail. Whatever she was pissed about was sure to come out sooner or later because she isn't one to hold shit in. But damn... if she knew about last night or even suspected... What if she came straight out and asked me? Could I bring myself to tell her the truth or would I have the balls to look her in the eyes and tell her a lie?

I tried not to think about that. There was no way that she could have known. I decided at that moment to do something nice for her. I got on-line and ordered her favorite bouquet of flowers from a nearby boutique. She loved orchids. I would send the orchids to her and give her a romantic evening to make up for cancelling our plans from the night before. Instead of ordering one bouquet, I ordered two and paid extra to have them delivered by the time she got home.

The day went by smoothly with hardly any contact with Candice and minimum tension between me and my boy. Darnell and I actually had lunch together and laughed and joked as we usually did, making plans to shoot some hoops Friday after work. I lingered behind Candice and Darnell when they left not wanting to be caught in the elevator with her again in case she tried some booty popping shit again.

Yani

I made my way home and was surprised to see Tierra's Range Rover wasn't in the driveway. It was after 7pm and she's normally always home before me. I went inside and began gagging when I smelled the stench of burnt food. What in the hell is going on?

"Tianna and Tamia! What the hell is that smell?"

Tianna came down the stairs shaking her head. "Daddy, Tamia's trying to kill us calling herself cooking in here," she burst out laughing.

"At least I tried you little troll. If it weren't for me, you'd be eating peanut butter and jelly," Tamia sneered at her little sister.

Tianna rolled her eyes, "A PJB sandwich would be an upgrade from the gruel you tried to serve up."

"Hey!" I shouted to get them quiet. "Close your mouths, now." My girls piped down after giving each other the evil eye. "Tianna, open some windows in here. Tamia, where is your mother?"

Tamia shrugged her shoulders. "I don't know. She came back briefly after her meeting earlier and then left right back out."

I frowned. What the hell was going on with my wife? "Wait, she left back out? How long ago was this?"

"After she dropped Tianna and J.R off. This was like after 4 o' clock. We were hungry so I tried to bake some chicken and make some baked potatoes and string beans," Tamia said as she made her way to the kitchen. I followed behind her.

"Yeah and she burned the potatoes and string beans because she was too busy yapping on her phone," Tianna said as she pushed up a window in the dining room.

"Say something else…" Tamia said in a menacing tone.

Tianna turned around to face her. "And what're you going to do? I ain't Brittany."

"You know what, I'm about to knock the hell outta both of y'all. Tamia, it's okay just dump the food in the trash. I'll order us a pizza. Tianna, is your homework done?"

"No, she was too busy playing that stupid Xbox," Tamia rolled her eyes.

"Shut up!" Tianna shot back.

"Both of you shut up! Damn, y'all are like Itchy and Scratchy in here. The two of you better learn to get along and fast. You treat your friends better than you treat each other and I'm sick of it. Next one of you who opens your

170

mouths, you'll be sucking soup through a straw for the rest of the month, I'ma smack you so damn hard," I threatened. "Tianna, you know damn well you don't touch that game until after you finish your homework. Get upstairs and get your homework done and you better not touch that Xbox for the rest of the week, you understand me?"

"Awww Dad!" Tianna whined.

"Do you understand me?!" I asked louder.

"Yes sir," she sulked as she made her way upstairs. Tamia snickered. I glared at her.

"As for you, give me that damn phone."

"Huh?" Tamia asked with her eyes wide.

"Huh my ass. Running your mouth on that damn phone, you could have set the whole damn house on fire. Sometimes you act like you can't do anything else when you have that damn phone to your ear. Give it up. Your ass is suspended. Regardless if the fight wasn't your fault, you're still in trouble."

Tamia handed me the phone looking as though she was going to cry and I snatched it from her. She plopped down on the steps and crossed her arms over her chest. "This sucks. When is Mom coming home?"

I looked down at Tamia with eyes so cold I swore I saw her shiver. She got the message and quickly disappeared upstairs to her room. I looked around and sighed. So this is what Tierra goes through with keeping these girls in line. Where the hell was my wife?

I dialed the pizza place from Tamia's phone and began pacing the living room when I saw the trashcan. Inside were the orchids that I purchased for her earlier. She threw my flowers in the damn trash… Oh shit… she knows.

Fear washed over me as I ordered the pizzas for the kids. I sat down going over in my head what I would tell her, what excuse I could come up with or how I could cover my tracks. Damn… I fucked up big time and at that moment I feared I would probably lose my wife for good.

The pizza arrived and I paid for it, leaving the delivery man a nice tip. It was now after 8pm and Tierra still hadn't gotten home. I ate dinner with the kids and played Michael Jackson's Dance Experience and Guitar Hero on the Wii with them. I had fun with them and it had been a while since I sat down and actually played at home with them. By 9:30pm, I sent them all to take their showers and get ready for bed. Tianna and J.R continuously asked where their mother was. The only thing I could think to tell them was that she was working late and would be home when they woke up in the morning.

Before Tamia went to bed, she knocked on the bedroom door. It was just after 10pm and Tierra still wasn't home. I wasn't sure if I should be pissed or scared. I think scared would suit me just fine. I was going to lose my wife. My wife was leaving me. Here I was doing what she had done numerous times; sitting at home, watching the clock, checking my phone for a text or phone call, wondering where she was and when she would be home. Wondering if I should call her or just sit and wait. Here I was getting a taste of my own medicine and this shit was nasty and hard to swallow.

"Come in," I said. Tamia opened my door and gave me a hug. That was a rarity. I thought she was sucking up to get her phone back.

"I had a lot of fun tonight, Dad. We should do that more often," Tamia said after letting me go.

"I had a lot of fun too, baby-girl. And yeah, we will do it more often."

Tamia twisted her mouth as if she was thinking on what to say next. "Mom is mad at you…" she said as she looked at the floor.

"How do you figure?" I asked my daughter wondering if my wife had said anything to her about her recent behavior.

"Well for one, she didn't cook breakfast this morning, she threw your flowers in the trash and she isn't home now. Mom always cooks breakfast, she loves orchids and loves when you surprise her with flowers and she never comes home late."

My daughter was very perceptive. I nodded my head and sighed. "Yeah… she's upset." That was all I could think to say to Tamia.

"How come? Did you guys have a fight?" Tamia asked.

I hesitated for a moment. "Grown-up stuff, Tamia. Nothing to worry about. Go to bed, and I'll see you in the morning."

Tamia nodded and went over to my bedroom door. She stopped before leaving out and said without looking at me, "Fix it, please. I don't want to grow up in a house

174

without both of my parents." And with those words, she left the room and closed the door behind her.

I sighed and leaned back on the bed with my hands clasped behind my head thinking of what I would say to Tierra when she finally came home. I didn't mean to, but I nodded off.

I woke up a couple of hours later. I blinked as I waited for my vision to adjust to the lighting in the bedroom and then looked at my watch. It was almost 1am and my bed was still empty. I checked my phone and there was still no text message or phone call from Tierra. Now I was worried. I got out of the bed and checked downstairs. Her Range Rover was in the driveway behind my Acura. But where the hell was she? I checked the foyer, living room and the den. She was in neither of those rooms. I checked Tamia's and Tianna's rooms and she wasn't in there either. Lastly I checked J.R's room and there I found her sleeping in a fetal position next to our son. I sighed deeply and went over to her, tapping her lightly on shoulder.

"Baby, will you come to bed please? Let's talk."

Tierra waved my hand away. "Leave me alone," she said in a voice that I could tell was distorted from crying.

175

I knelt in front of her and stared at her for a moment feeling horrible that I had caused this kind of pain with my wife. But we could get through this. If she would just talk to me and listen to me and let me explain, we could get through this.

I eased my arms under her and pulled her into my arms so I could carry her to our bedroom. I was shocked that she didn't resist me. I carried her to our bedroom and used my foot to close the door before sitting on the bed with her in my arms. She put her hands to her face and cried. I shushed her as I stroked her hair and the side of her face.

"Baby, what's wrong?" I asked her.

Tierra took a few deep breaths as she tried to calm down and then shook her head. "I just want to go to bed, Markel."

"No Tee, something is going on with you. You've been acting real different lately. And you threw the flowers I bought for you in the trash. What's up? Talk to me, babe."

Tierra looked at me for a space of heartbeats before finally speaking. "Are you cheating on me?"

Yani

My heart raced as I thought of an answer. Tell the truth and risk losing her or tell a lie? Truth or lie? Whoever said there's no such thing as an honest lie, never told a brutal truth. So I looked my wife in the eyes and I lied.

"No, no I'm not cheating on you. Why would you ask me something like that?" I said to her.

She searched my face as if she were looking for something while thinking of what to say next. "Last night, when we had sex… it was like… it was like you were fucking me… like some cheap whore and not like your wife."

"What are you talking about?" I asked confused.

"Whenever we make love, no matter how freaky we do it, we never have sex in the dark. And we always end it facing each other. But last night, you fucked me in the dark, bent over like I was some random whore and not your wife and that's exactly what it made me feel like; like a cheap whore… like some random, cheap whore." Tierra sniffed as the tears fell from her eyes.

I closed my eyes and shook my head. I knew exactly what she was talking about. And she was right. "I'm sorry, babe. That wasn't my intention, trust me when I tell you that. I thought you were sleep when I got in the bed and the light was already out. You started grinding on me and kinda threw me off. I was dog tired from work and everything we did that morning and the night before. I had already messed up our evening by cancelling our dinner plans. I didn't want to ruin your mood…" I didn't know what else to say so I just shrugged and shook my head.

"So you gave me pity dick…?" Tierra asked as she frowned.

"No… no babe, never that. I was just tired. I'm sorry. I promise you that I've never seen you as a cheap whore and I would never treat you like that. Last night will never happen again, I promise." Tierra continued to search my face before finally giving in and nodding her head. I kissed her softly as I rubbed the back of her neck.

"Not having you here tonight made me realize I need to be home more and spend more time with the kids as well as you. I've been so focused on establishing a good life for us that I've been neglecting you and I don't want to do that anymore. I'm going to do better, I promise." Tierra nodded and I kissed her longingly. I thought she had me cold. And man, I was glad that she didn't. But fucking around with Candice and trying to cover my tracks ended up causing my wife to feel like a whore. I had to make up for that.

I undressed Tierra and made love to her with more passion than I knew existed in me. Sometimes some good dick can smooth things over with your woman. But I didn't just want to put a band aid over our problems by laying some pipe. I knew what I needed to do to make sure my woman felt like she was my one and only woman, my Queen, my everything. I was prepared to man up and do those things.

Tierra snuggled close to me and rested her head on my chest. I wrapped my arm around her and held her tightly. When she fell asleep, I watched her and listened to her breathe. I had the love of my life lying in my arms. No amount of pussy could replace the love Tierra gave to me endlessly.

16

Tierra

Markel looked me in my damn face and lied like shit. I came straight out and asked him if he cheated on me and he said no, lying with a straight face. I don't know why I expected him to tell me the truth. He must don't realize his back looks like a cat used it as a scratching post. I know back scratches from dick action when I see them and I damn sure didn't put them there. Nevertheless, I laid in his arms as his wife.

I know a lot of women would say, "Oh no, you should've left that nigga. He's this and he's that and he doesn't respect you and yadda yadda yadda." Honestly, until a woman has been in my situation; until she has put in the kind of time, love and commitment that I've put into this marriage, into this relationship for the last 16 years, no woman can say what she would have done. The shit is much easier said than done. Besides, we have children and I know how much it would hurt them if they saw us fighting or we separated and got a divorce. Their needs and what was best for them trumped my frivolous pride.

My pride... it was all but shattered as well as my dignity after I left Xavier's home. As good as the sex was, that pay back I called myself getting because of what Markel did to me did nothing for me except make me feel petty and cheap. It was one thing to get some payback dick when I was 19 and 20 years old. It was another thing to do it at 30. The first thing I was going to do in the morning was refund Xavier his money back and let him know what happened between us was wrong and will never happen again and it will be in our best interests if we don't see each other again on a professional or personal level.

The morning after Markel and I had our reconciliation, I fixed my children a magnificent breakfast of scrambled cheese eggs, bacon and red velvet pancakes. At the risk of going into the office late, Markel sat at the breakfast table with us and we all ate together. It was the first time in a long time, except when we sit down to eat dinner, that it felt like I had an actual family. Tianna and J.R were taken to school by Markel and

Tamia and I went to have a mother/daughter day at the hair and nail salon.

Everything was fine until I was in my Range Rover with Tamia on our way back from doing a little shopping when a call came through on my cell phone. Instead of answering on the headset, I answered through the Bluetooth to the truck.

"Tierra Davis' phone," I answered as I stopped at a red light.

"Hello beautiful," I heard Xavier's voice come on the line sounding just as sensuous and sexy as before. Frightened, I glanced quickly at Tamia who looked at me wide-eyed. "I'm sorry, you have the wrong number," I said before disconnecting the call.

"Who was that, Mom? He sounded like a whole creep," Tamia said with a frown on her face.

"Yeah, he did sound like a creep. He definitely had the wrong number," I said as my heart raced in my chest. The light turned green and I pulled off, feeling so nervous that I was positive my hands were shaking.

Knowing that Xavier would call back, I shut off the Bluetooth and placed my phone on vibrate. When we got in the house, I sent Tamia to her room to put away the new things that I bought for her.

I went inside of the den and closed the door for privacy so I could call Xavier back.

"What was that all about?" Xavier asked without saying hello when he answered.

"You called my business phone speaking socially and flirting while my daughter was in the car with me and the Bluetooth was on in my truck. Not cool, Xavier," I said as I paced inside of our den.

"Oh my bad, boo. I just wanted to hear your sexy voice and see if we could meet up this evening for another taste testing." The way he said that sounded so erotic, I immediately became aroused. I shook my head.

"That can't happen. What happened between us yesterday can never happen again." I said trying to sound as convincing as possible even though my mind was already reminiscing on how he ate my pussy after long stroking the fuck outta me. Yes, I was very aroused at that moment.

"Why not?" Xavier asked, sounding confused. "I know you're married and everything but, obviously not happily married if you was down with us making love yesterday."

I almost gagged, not because what he said repulsed me, but because he caught me off guard. The southern bitch in me surfaced. "Xavier, we did not make love. We fucked. And we fucked because I allowed a personal issue I had with my husband to cloud my better judgment. But that issue has been resolved now and we are okay. I can't see you like that again."

It was quiet on the phone for a brief moment and I wasn't sure if Xavier was going to call me an adulterous whore and demand his money back or what. Finally he said, "I understand. I'll send you an email with what we would like on the menu for the birthday party for my mother along with the number of guests."

I ran my finger across my forehead. "In my professional opinion, I think it would be best if you went with another catering company. I can send you some references along with a full refund…"

"That won't be necessary," Xavier said, interrupting me.

"Yes, it is necessary," I replied back.

"Like you said Mrs. Davis, we fucked. No big deal. And there is no point in letting personal issues interfere with your business."

We were silent again. I took a deep breath and went against my better judgment. "I'll be on the lookout for your email. Is there anything else I can assist you with today?" I asked in my professional voice.

"No, that will be all, Mrs. Davis. Have a blessed evening."

I quickly disconnected the call and closed my eyes as I leaned my head back. That could have been worse... a lot worse.

That night, I made a garden salad with Chicken Marsala, rice and string beans for me and my family. Markel came home on time and we all sat down and ate dinner together, laughing and talking about our days' events. Everything was cool until Tamia opened her mouth about the phone call I got in the car earlier.

"Oh, tell Dad about the creep that called your phone while we were out, Mom," Tamia giggled.

I gagged as I swallowed back some red wine and then wiped my mouth on a napkin.

"What creep?" Markel asked with a slight smile as he looked from Tamia to me.

"We were in the car earlier coming back from King of Prussia Mall when a call came through on Mom's Bluetooth. And when she answered, some dude sounding like a fake Rico Suave answered talking about some, hey beautiful." Tamia burst out laughing after imitating Xavier. Tianna and I chuckled with her.

"Who was he?" Markel asked with a brief chuckle.

I shrugged my shoulders. "I have no idea. I just told him he obviously had the wrong number and hung up. He must've realized he did because he didn't call back," I said casually as I cut into my chicken breast.

"I remember a chick sent me a text message talking all about how drunk she had gotten at the club the night before and fell asleep on her neighbor's porch thinking it was hers. I texted her back and said: You must still be drunk because you got the wrong number," Markel said. We laughed at the dinner table. But the way Markel looked at me was almost as though he was suspicious of the mystery man who called my phone.

We played board games and cards for a few hours until it was time for the kids to shower and head to bed.

186

Yani

Markel and I relaxed on the sofa, watching old movies like we used to when we were teenagers. We talked and joked around and for once, it felt like I had my husband and not just a business partner. He truly was the love of my life.

Things were going smoothly with us for the next month. Tamia was back in school. She and Tianna were finally getting along better than before. I did my cooking segment on the Rachel Ray's Morning Show and received rave reviews as well as a few new contracts. I also received a bonus check for the gala I catered in Delaware for an addition $10,000. With all of the jobs that were coming my way, I used that as an excuse to get out of the job I was requested to do by Xavier. I sent him an email explaining the cancellation due to my schedule and my need to travel outside of the city. I also sent him a full refund and a list of references for caterers who were equally as talented as I am as well as reasonably priced. He wasn't too happy with that and repeatedly made demands to see me so we could talk it over. Sorry homie, there's nothing to talk about.

As far as I could tell, Markel was back to being completely faithful to me again. No more late nights and suspicious scratches on his back. We even went for a romantic getaway to Puerto Rico for four days. The color of the golden brown sand and the warm, pale blue sea water was absolutely beautiful. He catered to me the entire time we were out, running me bubble baths, candle light dinners. I woke up our second morning there to a bed covered in rose pedals with some of the rose pedals leading to our suite's Jacuzzi. He was attentive to my wants while we were away and that made me love him even more. If it weren't for the kids, I wished we could stay there forever. Life was becoming beautiful just the way I always imagined it would be once we got married. But when everything is going good and you're thinking life is good, life laughs out loud and says back, "Not so fast bitch, give me a second." Shit started getting real two days after we had gotten home.

Xavier called my phone. I saw his number and rolled my eyes as I shook my head. "Tierra Davis' phone," I answered, trying to mask my annoyance with him.

"Tierra I need to see you," Xavier said into the phone without speaking.

Yani

"Xavier, I already explained to you…" I started to say but he interrupted me.

"This has nothing to do with what happened between the two of us. It was a one-time mistake that will never happen again. I'm over it. But there is no other caterer that has satisfied me or comes close to being able to pull together a menu like you and my mother's party is in three weeks. Can we please put what happened between us aside and put this thing together? I had already told my family about you and how delicious your food was and they saw you on Rachel Ray's Morning Show. I don't want them to think I made the story up about how we met in the winery to make it seem like I knew someone just because they appeared on TV. Please don't make me look like a fool in front of my family," Xavier practically begged.

I took a deep breath and against my better judgment, I gave in. "Okay, I'll move some things around in my schedule and squeeze you in. Send the menu to me again via email with the rest of the information," I told him.

"Well, after I told my sister about you and she saw your cooking segment on TV, she wanted to do a taste testing as well. I don't mind sending the original $200 to you along with an additional $200 for her."

"That won't be necessary. When is she available?" I asked.

"Tomorrow is her only day off so is it possible we could meet around the same time at my place?"

I paused not liking the way that sounded. The last time I was at his house, I was cumming all over his face after getting my pussy licked. I told myself it was just revenge sex and I could be around him without anything happening. Besides, his sister would be there. Everything would be cool.

"Yes, I will be there around one tomorrow afternoon with the food samples. Is there anything else I can assist you with?"

"No, that will be all Mrs. Davis," Xavier said in a non-flirtatious manner. I told him to have a good day and disconnected the call.

The next day, I made my way back to his house and became extremely hot over his appearance. Even though it was casual, the plain gray, long sleeved top framed his athletic torso and muscular arms. He had grown his beard a bit but kept it cut closely to his face as it outlined his jaw. His black sweat pants were oversized, but fit perfectly showcasing his bubble-butt ass. I couldn't help thinking about grabbing it and squeezing it as he pumped his dick in and out of me. *"Stop it, Tierra!"* I chastised myself.

Xavier carried the trays and burners in the house as he did before and I followed him inside. I looked around expecting to see his sister, but saw no one. He must have read my mind because he said, "My sister is running a little late. She works as an at home care person and her relief hasn't come yet. She said she will be here as soon as she can."

I nodded my head as I began setting up. "Okay," I said softly. I could feel his eyes on me just as before and I was becoming nervous. I pulled my hair behind my ear as I tried ignoring the way he watched me. He came over to me as if to get a closer look but stood behind me, standing so close that his pelvic area was pressed against my backside. I could feel his erection growing against my ass and smell his aftershave and cologne. Damn, this man smelled good enough to eat. I could feel my chest getting hot as well as in between my legs. Oh no, not again...

"You are absolutely gorgeous, Mrs. Davis," Xavier said close to my ear. My eyes fluttered at the sound of his voice. I made myself remember my husband and eased away from him.

"Xavier, I didn't come here for this. You know I'm married," I said to him as I looked him in his eyes. Sexy... dark... dreamy, bedroom eyes. Damn you, Zane!

"Yes but are you happy?" Xavier asked as he stepped closer to me slowly. I backed away and bumped into the table. Shit, no-where to run.

"Yes, I am..." I said as he pressed his body to mines. I could feel his hand trace up the small of my back as he used his other hand to run his fingers through my hair.

"You sure about that?" He leaned in to kiss me and I tried to stop him. Okay... I tried a teeny weeny bit to stop him. Common sense told me to stop. But my pussy said, fuck that! He kissed me softly, the tip of his tongue tracing over my mouth before slipping inside. His lips were so artistic in the manner in which he kissed me that I stopped resisting and kissed him back. Before I knew it, I was in his bedroom sitting on the edge of the bed with my skirt pulled up above my hips and my panties on his floor while his face was between my legs, licking and sucking on my pussy again. I placed my hand on the back of his head as I leaned my head back and moaned out loud. He slipped two fingers inside of my ass making me squeal and I came so hard. The orgasm left me shaking, trembling and panting as I struggled to catch my breath. But that shit had to stop there. I jumped up and grabbed my panties.

"Where are you going?" Xavier asked. I looked back at him and saw that big, black, Mandingo dick sticking out of his sweatpants. Oh lord, let me get the fuck outta here before I mount this man and fuck him like a porn star. I hurriedly put my panties on.

"This is wrong. This is wrong! I can't do this again. And your sister could be here any minute," I said as I straightened out my clothes.

"She isn't coming. She sent a text message when we first got up here…"

The look on my face stopped Xavier dead in his tracks. "She isn't coming?" I thought for a moment and didn't remember seeing him check his phone when we came up here. He lied about the whole thing. His sister was never coming. I looked at him with fire in my eyes.

"You sonuva bitch," I said as I shook my head.

"Wait, Tierra…" Xavier said as I hurried from the bedroom. He followed me downstairs and I began packing up my trays and burners. "This wasn't a set-up, I really wanted to see you. And she does want to taste your food."

"No, you lied. She wasn't coming and you knew it! This was just your way to get me back in bed with you."

"Tierra, listen to me. Okay… yes… I wanted to make love to you again. Can you blame me? I'm attracted to you, I won't lie about that. And I know you're married. But I can't help how I feel about you."

"You don't even know me," I said to him as I began marching to his front door.

"But I'm trying to get to know you if you would just let me."

I ignored him as I loaded up my truck. I was getting ready to get in when he grabbed my arm to stop me. I yanked away.

"Tierra, I'm sorry if you feel like I deceived you. But I really do want to see where things can go with us. I think you're an incredible woman, extremely gorgeous and you deserve to be treated better than how your husband treats you," Xavier said to me as he held my hand. I snatched it away.

"You don't know a thing about my husband and don't you dare make assumptions about my marriage. This thing that happened between us is over. Do not call me again. Do not contact me again. Find another caterer and stay the hell away from me." I got in my truck and pulled off.

I couldn't believe he tried some slick shit like that! What I couldn't believe more is that I fell for it when something inside of me knew that he was up to something. Even worse, I cheated on my husband and this time, it wasn't revenge.

I don't know what came over me, but my eyes became watery and the tears began to fall before I had a chance to stop them. I felt like a cheating, adulterous whore that couldn't keep my panties up and this wasn't like me at all. I pulled up to the corner of 15th street to make a right turn when a black Chevy Equinox pulled up next to me to make a left turn. The stupid bitch was blocking my damn view so I pulled up some more to see if I was clear to make my turn and then pulled off. I was about to put on some music when I noticed the Equinox made a right turn behind me instead of the left turn they were originally set to make. And the bitch was driving super-fast behind me. Today ain't the day to be on some bull-shit. I will knock a bitch smooth the fuck out. I looked in my rear-view mirror to see if she was going to hit me since she was driving so fast behind me but she didn't. Smart girl. When the light changed, I made my left turn before on-coming traffic could come through. Half of the way down the street, I looked into my rearview mirror and this bitch made a left turn and was speeding down the street behind me. I suddenly had a feeling this bitch was about to do something stupid. How right I was. I saw where she was inching over to the left to try to go around me and cut me off which was not necessary, so I eased over to the left to force her into on-coming traffic. Oh bitch, you want to play *Need for Speed,* I got something for your ass. Cars were coming towards her in oncoming traffic as she was next to me, blaring on their horns and I sped up so she couldn't get around. I heard her brakes as she slowed down and jumped back behind me. I thought that near death experience would have humbled her monkey-ass but no, ole girl decided to do it on the right side. She sped up next to me and then swerved in front of me and hit the brakes almost causing me to hit the back of her car. No this bitch didn't! And then she sped off. Heh, momma didn't raise no punk-bitch and today ain't the day. I chased after her ass and caught her at a red light. I pulled my car in front of hers horizontally, blocking her in as someone was pulling up behind us and I jumped out of my truck.

"Bitch, have you lost your muthafucking mind?!" I screamed at her. "Get the fuck outta the car! I'ma beat your ass today!"

She was mouth all mighty inside that car but I guess Chevy neglects to auto lock their doors when in motion. I opened her door and snatched that bitch by her hair and commenced to kicking her ass. She could have caused me to get into an accident. Having a seatbelt on left her at a disadvantage though she tried desperately to get a few punches in. She finally got the seatbelt off and fell out of her little mini jeep, but I was on her ass like white on rice. Cars honked their horns at us and people got out of their cars to watch us fight. I had that bitch by her collar, and was giving her the business North Philly style. She had me fucked up pulling some road rage shit like that.

Next thing I knew, a cop was grabbing me and hemming me up against my Range Rover.

"Ma'am, calm down right now!" the officer practically yelled in my face.

"You cheap whore! I know you're fucking my husband. You nasty bitch, wait until I get my hands on you!"

I was out of breath and looked around the cop. "Bitch, I don't even know your husband! You damn near caused me to crash my truck getting me confused with someone else. I should beat your ass again!"

The cop pushed me into the car advising me to calm down again.

"I saw you leaving our home, bitch! Don't act like you don't know my husband when I just saw you outside with Xavier!"

My heart pounded in my chest so loudly I was positive the cop could hear it. Wife…? This nigga told me he wasn't involved! Here he was hounding me over some pussy and had a whole wife! I was kicking the wrong ass. I needed to kick his fucking ass!

"Ma'am is it true? Are you sleeping with her husband?" the officer asked me.

Yani

"He hired me for a catering job but there was nothing going on between us," I lied as I fixed my clothes.

The officer looked at me as though he didn't believe me. "Well I'm going to have to take the both of you down to the station to get this sorted out."

"This bitch almost caused me to crash my car pulling that shit back there and could've caused a head on collision with herself and another driver! Are you serious?" I shouted.

"And you started a fight in the middle of a busy intersection, approached her at her vehicle and assaulted her. She could press charges if she wants to."

I couldn't believe this shit. The nigga lied about being married. Because of that, his wife tried to run me off the fucking road. And now this cop is slapping handcuffs on me and putting me in the back of a fucking police wagon. Just when you think it's safe to be happy, life fucks around and fucks it all up for you. How the hell was I going to explain this shit to Markel? Damn it!

17

Markel

Imagine my surprise when I get a phone call telling me my wife has been arrested in Delaware for aggravated assault. They must have the wrong Tierra Davis because my wife wouldn't be in Delaware assaulting anybody. But no, they had the right woman. I called Darnell into my office as I gathered my things so I could leave early.

"What's up, Mar?" Darnell spoke as he stood in my doorway.

"Today is your lucky day. You've always complained about me not giving you any additional patients. Today you get to do a paraffin bath on Mrs. Gibson who is coming in with acute pain in her wrist's joints. You will also handle a few heating treatments. Candice will give you the patients' charts. I have to leave early," I said to Darnell hurriedly as I threw on my peat coat and grabbed my scarf.

"Is everything okay?" Darnell asked.

Yani

I took a deep breath not really wanting to tell Darnell what was going on but figured he's been my boy for so long now that it wasn't a problem. We probably would laugh about it over drinks once I got the entire story from Tierra.

"Tierra was arrested for aggravated assault out in Delaware."

Darnell looked at me with wide eyes and then cracked a grin. "You can take a chick out the ghetto but you can't take the ghetto out the chick." He burst out laughing. I found myself chuckling with him.

"Not funny, man. I gotta head over to Delaware to see what the hell is going on. I'll tell you what's up later," I said to Darnell as I slapped him a handshake before leaving.

I hopped in my Acura and cranked the heat up. Damn, it was freezing outside. Winter was not playing this year. I wondered who Tierra had knocked the hell out and why. Just when I thought everything was good with her and we were good, she pulls a stunt like this.

Though I tried my hardest to stop, I was still sleeping with Candice. What made it even worse was that I was lying to my colleagues claiming that I had important lunches and meetings that I had to attend to when really I was sneaking off to hotel rooms and having all kinds of wild sex with Candice. This girl had some serious deep throating skills. What made the sex so hot with Candice was she was open to pleasing me in any way I wanted to be pleased in. I didn't have to ask her to give me some head. Most times during our drive to the hotel, she would put her head in my lap and start sucking the dick on the spot. I knew I was wrong. I knew I was dead wrong, but it was something about her that made it hard for me to resist her. I felt so bad about the affair I was having with Candice that I took Tierra to Puerto Rico for four days in hopes that would cure this insatiable appetite I have for fucking my assistant. It didn't. The day after I came back, we were in my office fucking after everyone left for the day.

I made it over to Delaware almost an hour and a half after leaving the office because traffic was so heavy. I stopped at the help desk to let the clerk know who I was there for.

"May I ask why she is being held?" I asked the clerk politely. I got the feeling she was drawn to me by the way she smiled and licked her lips at me.

"Apparently there was some road rage issue brought on by a woman who claimed your wife was sleeping with her husband," the clerk explained to me. The room went silent. Wait… did she just say what I think she just said. My wife got into a fight because she was fucking another woman's husband? She was cheating on me? Nah man! This better be a muthafucking mistake!

"Where is she now?" I asked in a surprisingly calm tone.

The clerk pointed behind me. "Here she comes now."

I turned around and looked at my wife as she made her way over to me. She didn't look scared or concerned in the slightest. She better have a real good fucking explanation about what the fuck this shit was all about. I know muthafucking well another nigga wasn't running up in my wife!

Tierra looked at me and then went over to the clerk's desk to retrieve her things.

"Mrs. Jenkins will not be pressing any charges. She states that it was a misunderstanding and she jumped to conclusions when she saw you leaving their home earlier," I overheard the clerk saying to my wife.

203

"I was only there for business. My relationship with Mr. Jenkins is strictly professional. But she needs to know, jumping to conclusions could've gotten me killed and caused her to get that ass beat." My wife snatched up her things and walked away. I watched her mean-ass stroll and caught a boner. But something about the idea of my wife being arrested for assault and accused of cheating with another woman's husband didn't sit well with me. I followed her out to my car.

"You wanna tell me what the hell is going on?" I asked Tierra as we walked out of the police station.

"Nothing to tell. The bitch wrongly accused me of cheating with her husband. She pulled some road rage shit on the street, almost caused me to crash and I beat that ass. Case closed," Tierra replied as if it were no big deal.

"Why would she think something like that if your relationship was only professional?" I asked. Something didn't sound right with her story. I know women can be paranoid at times, but if it was strictly business she wouldn't have tried to run my wife off the road.

"I don't know! Maybe she's one of those paranoid bitches that always think people are up to no good.

204

Psycho bitch." Tierra got in my car and slammed the door. I climbed in with her.

"You sure there's nothing else you want to tell me?" I asked her as I started the car.

Tierra looked me in my eyes and I swear I saw hate. "You sure there's nothing you want to tell me?" she asked back.

I looked at her for a moment wondering what she meant by that and shook my head. "I'm not doing this with you, tonight."

"Good then don't," Tierra snapped back.

"Ay yo, lose the fucking attitude. I just had to leave my job early to come get your ass outta jail."

"And who the fuck are you talking to like that, Markel?!" Tierra screamed back. "I didn't need you to come get me. They were releasing me. I know how to find my way back to my truck and get home just fine without you."

I shook my head again as I started driving away. Maybe this is why I was fucking Candice. Easy like Sunday morning. No fighting, no arguments, no drama. Just fuck and roll. "Your attitude's been real fucked up lately."

"Maybe you should ask yourself why my attitude's been real fucked up lately," Tierra shot back.

"Man whatever," I replied.

"I know it's the fuck whatever," Tierra said back. She always had to have the last word and that shit was annoying. Fine, she wanted the last word, she could have it. I turned the radio up to tune her out. She turned it down.

"Yo, don't touch my shit," I snapped at her.

"I don't want to hear that shit right now, Markel. I have a fucking headache."

"That's on you," I said as I turned it back up. She turned it back down. "Yo what the fuck is your problem? You got an issue with how I listen to music in my car, get the fuck out and walk." I didn't mean to say that last part but she was getting on my nerves. And I honestly didn't believe nothing was going on with whoever this new client was. Shit if I were him and was trying to keep my dirt on the down low, I would have went with the story of our relationship being strictly business too.

"Stop the fucking car," Tierra said.

I pulled over at the next corner and Tierra got out, slamming my door behind herself. That's the second time she slammed my fucking door. I rolled her window down. "Tee, where the hell are you going?" I asked her as she marched down the street. She stuck her middle finger up at me and kept walking. Fuck it then. Let her ass walk. I rolled her window up and sped off. Tierra was on some other time and whatever time that was, I definitely didn't have time for it. I called Candice on the Bluetooth to the Acura and waited for her to answer. Two rings later and her sexy voice came in over the speakers.

"Yes Mr. Davis," Candice purred through her phone. My dick always got hard when she said that. Sometimes while we were fucking, I would have her call me Mr. Davis. That shit was sexy as hell.

"Hey baby, I'm on my way back to the office. Tell Darnell he can go ahead and leave," I told her.

"Okay," she replied before disconnecting the call. I needed my dick sucked badly and she was definitely the right woman for the job.

I got back to the office and everyone was gone, thankfully. Practically all of the lights were out except for the lamp on my desk. Candice was in my office leaned back on my desk with her shirt unbuttoned exposing her sexy, black and silver laced underwire bra. I went in and sat down in my desk chair still feeling the sting from me and Tierra's argument. I needed some relief really badly.

Candice stood in front of me and ran her hands over the freshly cut waves to my hair as she leaned close to me. Another thing that I liked about Candice was that she never asked me questions about my wife or family. She knew she was my side piece and she stayed in her lane like a side chick should. She had that pussy on standby when I needed or wanted it and never gave me any drama.

I ran my hands up the back of her thigh until I found my way underneath her skirt. I gently squeezed on her soft, round ass cheeks as I kissed her navel, slowly swirling my tongue around it and licked her stomach as I peeled down her panties. I squeezed her ass again, rolling her cheeks around my palms before standing up so I could kiss her. We played tongue tag with each other as she undid the buckle to my belt and pulled my pants down so she could unleash my throbbing dick from the confines of my boxers. She took my place in my desk chair and her wet, warm mouth wrapped around my cock, letting it slide as far as she could get it into her mouth before she gagged a little. I loved the way she looked up at me with those grayish blue eyes, seeing those pink, pouty lips wrapped around my dark meat as her head and mouth moved back and forth. Damn, I needed this. I ran my fingers through her hair, wrapping it around my wrist and began to slowly slide my dick in and out of her mouth. She kept up with my rhythm as her sucking and slurping made harmonic sounds with minor gags in between. Those wet sucking noises she was making made my balls tight and my toes curled just a bit in my dress shoes. I needed to feel that pussy around my dick.

I stood Candice up and kissed her long and hard as I sat back in the chair with her straddling me. I popped out her petite, firm tits with those large pick nipples and sucked on them as I felt her warm, wet cunt slide down on my dick. I grabbed her by her hips and thrust myself inside of her making her moan and our movement began. I leaned the chair back a little so I could push myself deeper inside of her. Damn, her pussy was wet and tight. I pushed two of my fingers in her mouth and she sucked on them before we kissed, playing tongue tag some more. I could feel myself about to cum and pulled her all the way onto me as I groaned and grunted, cumming deep inside of her. We looked at each other and giggled before giving each other a brief kiss. Then I looked in my doorway...

Tierra was standing there watching us with her mouth gaped open and tears running down her face. I practically pushed Candice off of me making her fall to the floor and jumped up. Tierra backed away and ran from the office without saying anything.

"Tierra, wait!" I shouted. Without thinking, I tried to run after her but tripped over my pants that were still around my ankles and fell into one of the desks. "Shit!" I hollered out. I quickly pulled my pants up and ran from the office. Tierra was just getting on the elevator and I tried to hurry up and catch it but the doors closed in my face. I ran to the stairs and began going down, skipping two steps at a time, hoping that I made it to the garage before Tierra pulled off. I made it through the doors just as I heard her Range Rover screeching as she hurriedly pulled off.

"Fuck!" I exclaimed, out of breath. Shit, she caught me red handed. I patted my pocket for my keys and remembered they were in my coat pocket. I went over to the elevator so I could go back to my office.

By the time I had gotten back up there, Candice was gone. She must have been on the elevator going down as I was coming back up. I grabbed my cell phone and my car keys and ran back to the elevator. It seemed like it was taking forever in a damn day for it to hurry up and get back up there.

"Come the fuck on, man!" I shouted as I repeatedly mashed on the down button. I called Darnell from my cell phone.

"Yo homie, what's up?" Darnell answered after the first ring.

"Darnell, I need you to go by my house now," I said to him hastily as the elevator finally arrived.

"What's the matter Markel?" Darnell asked.

"I can't explain right now. Just go to my house and wait for me."

Darnell hesitated. "Alright, I'm on my way. I just walked in the door."

I disconnected the call. Fuck, fuck, fuck! Damn, my wife just caught me boning my damn assistant. In all the years I had messed around on Tierra, I never got caught.

How the fuck did I let that shit happen tonight? I needed to come up with a game plan and fast before I got to the house.

When I got to the house, Darnell was outside hugging Tianna. J.R was sitting in his car and Tamia looked as if she could kick my ass herself. Oh shit…

"What the fuck is going on?" Darnell asked me.

"What are they doing out here, it's freezing?" I asked Darnell. I took my coat off and wrapped it around Tamia. I could hear Tianna crying her eyes out as Darnell held her.

"Tierra is in there going the fuck off! She's smashing shit and throwing glasses, breaking shit up. What the fuck is up?"

I looked at Darnell and then looked at my kids not wanting to say what the problem was in front of them. "Hold up, I'll be right back." I took a deep breath and walked in my house. It looked like a bomb had been dropped on that bitch. Broken glass, shattered picture frames, torn photos, over turn tables, cut up sofa cushions. My heart raced in my chest. Was I scared? Hell muthafuckin yeah. I heard more glasses crashing upstairs and took another deep breath before making my way up there. Tierra was screaming but her words weren't audible. I could tell she was crying as well.

She must have heard me coming because a glass came flying in my direction and I ducked just in time.

"Tierra! Calm the fuck down!" I said to her.

"Calm down? CALM DOWN!!!" she screamed. She threw the fine China glasses that were given to us as a wedding gift more than ten years prior. Damn, I really liked those glasses. "You've been doing this shit to me for sixteen fucking years!! Sixteen fucking years and you want me to calm down?!" She stared at me with so much hate in her eyes that I could feel it in my stomach. The hate, anger and pain in her eyes were unlike anything I had ever seen before.

"Tierra, if you would just let me explain…" I tried to say.

"Explain what, Markel?! EXPLAIN WHAT! I ignored your whores for a long fucking time. I kept my mouth closed for a long fucking time. I figured if I became a better woman, if I became a better wife, you would see me as enough! But you're still doing this shit to me!" she screamed at me.

"Tierra, please…" was all that I could think to say.

"Here I was coming back to apologize thinking maybe I was too much of a bitch today and you're screwing your fucking assistant in your office barely an hour after you left me walking in the fucking cold!"

I was at a loss for words and didn't know what to say at first. "I never meant to hurt you."

Tierra laughed in my face. "Too late for that lame-ass shit Markel, you've been doing this shit since high-school. You've been fucking bitches behind my back all through high-school and college, coming home and kissing me after you've been kissing these bitches. Meanwhile I'm busting my fucking ass to hold it down for you. Everybody is laughing in my face and behind my back because they knew you were doing me dirty. But noooo. I had to trust in my man. I had to believe in my man. My dumb ass MARRIED MY MAN!" Tierra screamed as she smashed more glass.

"I asked you to your face were you cheating on me and you looked me in my face and you lied," she said as she trembled.

"I wasn't..." I said absent mindedly.

"AND YOU'RE STILL LYING!" she screeched. "I saw the fucking scratches on your back that morning and I didn't put them there because you were too busy giving me left over pity dick, fucking me like some whore you bent over!"

"Tierra, I understand you're upset. But if you could just calm down for a second and let me explain…" I tried to reason with her.

"Explain what, Markel? Huh? What the fuck do you have to explain? What the fuck do I have to listen to?" She fell silent as if she was granting me permission to speak my piece. I was still at a loss for words. "Do you love her?" she asked me.

"Huh?" I said as if I didn't hear her.

"Do you love her?" she asked me more slowly. I fumbled for an answer and she turned her back to me, groaning before she burst into tears. "I can't fucking believe you!" she cried with her hands to her face.

I walked over to her and tried to hug her but she knocked the horse-shit outta me.

"Don't you touch me! Don't you ever fucking touch me again or so help me God I will kill you." The look on Tierra's face let me know that she was not joking and chances are her threat was real. All I could do was look at her. I felt horrible for the pain I caused her. I felt absolutely terrible. And I was positive that this was the end for us and she was leaving me for sure.

"Get out…" she said, sounding exhausted and defeated.

"Tierra, we need to talk about this…" I tried to say.

"Get the fuck outta my house you sonuva bitch!!" she screamed.

I backed away from her and glanced around before leaving and going down the stairs. I went outside and called for the kids to come with me.

"Dad, where are we going?" Tamia asked me.

"We're gonna go to grandma's house for a little while, okay. Mommy needs some time alone."

Tianna was still hysterical when Darnell let her go. "I wanna stay with Mom," she sobbed as Darnell walked her to the car.

"Why can't we stay home?" J.R asked.

"Because Mom and Dad are fighting," Tamia looked at me with contempt as she sat in the back of the car. She put her arm around Tianna to comfort her as she looked out the window. I saw her try to wipe a tear from her own eyes and felt like shit. What have I done?

"Is everything cool, man? What's going on?" Darnell asked me before I got in the car.

"I can't talk right now. I'ma holla at you later, alright?" I said to Darnell as I got in the car.

Darnell smacked the hood of my car. "Alright my nigga, let me know if you need anything."

I didn't bother responding. I drove off and made my way to my mother's house. I needed to find a way to fix this and fast. I didn't want to lose my wife or break up my family. But I should've thought of that a little sooner. Tierra knew all along about my cheating. She never said anything, never confronted me, just continued to try to be a better woman in hopes she would be enough for me. I had never seen her show that kind of raw emotion in the sixteen years I had been with her. I had to fix this. I had to make it up to her. I owed her that.

18

Darnell

Like I said, what's done in the dark always comes to the light. I don't know what Markel did and who he did it with, but the shit finally caught up with his ass. I knew it was only a matter of time before it did. That's why I don't fucking understand for the life of me if he knew he liked having a variety of pussy, why the fuck would he go through the motions of marrying Tierra? He might look at me and think I'm not being a man because I haven't settled down, but I accept my reality. I like pussy. Ain't nothing better than some pussy except some new pussy. Don't get me wrong, when I wanted Tierra to leave Markel, I would have committed to her. I would have stopped chasing. As a matter of fact, the whole time we were messing around, she was the only chick I was hitting off. I wasn't fucking with no other bitches. Niggas be getting these chicks that be holding them down, being loyal as shit and know muthafucking well they don't have any intentions of being faithful to them. But to keep them from being with any other niggas, they'll fuck around and get them knocked up as a way to lock them down. And then some of them do the marrying shit just to keep a nigga that would probably treat her better from having her. It's the dumbest and most selfish fucking logic I'd ever heard of.

His words had gotten to me about the whole settling down bid. And I figured if I was going to settle down, I might as well do it with a chick who had her shit together, didn't have a bunch of fucking kids and was about more than her hair, nails, the latest fashion trend and wasn't in and out of bars. Even though I had hit Candice off so fucking easily, I knew she was a good girl. She did her work and stayed out of the bullshit. We went out a few times and messed around a bit after our first encounter. I couldn't see her as much as I wanted to because she was in school and Mar kept her so busy at the job. But when we did get to spend time together, sometimes she would sleep over at my crib or I would sleep over at hers. Candice was a good look. I was considering taking things seriously with her.

After Markel left, I went inside of the house. Holy muthafucking shit! Tierra set it the fuck off in this damn place. Shit was broken up, thrown everywhere, cut the fuck up. Yeah, Tierra definitely must've found out Markel was cheating on her again. But with who though, cause ole boy wasn't saying shit to me about who he was hitting off?

I went into the den and Tierra was standing by the fire place leaning over the top, sipping on a glass of red wine. Inside of the fireplace were wedding pictures that were burning and melting. Ironically, Mary J. Blige was playing on the stereo. *Not Gon' Cry*. Fitting for this moment.

"Don't do that Tee," I said to her, speaking of the burning wedding photos.

"You knew…" Tierra said as she looked at me through tear drenched eyes. As tired as she looked, she was still gorgeous to me.

"Knew what?" I asked her as I stepped over some broken glass.

"That he was cheating on me again," she replied before taking another drink.

"No. Honestly I didn't know he was messing around on you again. I thought after y'all got married, he threw his player's card in."

"Yeah, but you knew about all the other times though. You tried to warn me but noooo. My dumb ass didn't want to listen. I just had to stand by my man and try to keep my family together and for what? For what?" She shook her head and sniffed before taking another sip from her glass.

"You're a lot of things Tierra, but stupid ain't one of them," I said to her truthfully.

She smirked. "Then what do you call it? What woman with any self-respect, any dignity, any pride, would allow a man to cheat on her and disrespect her for over fifteen years?"

"A lot of women Tee," I said to her.

"Then maybe we all need to form a club called Real Dumb Bitches of Life."

"Cut that shit out, Tee." I took the glass from her and sat it on the mantel. She put her hands to her face and cried. Had this been college, I would have put my arms around her and held her. But I didn't think I should this time especially if I was considering taking things seriously with Candice.

"I can't believe he is still doing this to me. Like, what the fuck is wrong with me? Am I ugly? Do I suck in bed? Am I dumb or what? Like what the fuck is it? Why is it that I just never was enough for him and if I'm not enough, why the fuck didn't he just let me go? Instead of frauding all these years like I was the love of his life when obviously, I'm not." She sobbed and put her hands back to her face.

"I don't think it's a matter of Markel thinking you're not enough for him. And you know damn well you're not ugly. You've never been an ugly chick and far from stupid. And not to bring up old shit, but you're definitely not bad in bed so that definitely ain't it," I tried to reassure her.

"Then what the fuck is wrong with me?" Tierra asked angrily as she looked up at me.

"Maybe you should be asking what the fuck is wrong with him," I replied after a moment.

Tierra shook her head and grabbed for her glass again. She gulped down the rest of the red wine and poured herself another drink. "This is the fuck why I didn't want him to have a female assistant. If he was going to cheat on me, the least he could have done was cheat on me with a Black chick. Why the fuck did she have to be White? That's what the fuck I never understood about the bitches he cheated on me with. Most of those bitches were White. Blonde hair, blue eyed White bitches." She shook her head in contempt before taking another drink from her glass.

Hold the muthafucking phone… Markel was fucking Candice? You've gotta be fucking kidding me. Now the shit was coming together. The last minute meetings and conference calls, the lunches. That bitch wasn't too busy for me because of school; she was too busy fucking Markel. I finally come across a bitch I considered settling down with after his suggestion and this bitch was fucking my right hand man? See why I don't take these bitches seriously? And he was talking about me not fucking with Candice because he didn't want to risk a sexual harassment suit against the company when really it was because he was already fucking with her regardless the fact he already had a wife. This muthafucka was a piece of work.

"I'm surprised you didn't know he was fucking his assistant," Tierra said.

"No, I didn't know. Never would've suspected it," I replied blandly. Inside I was fucking heated. "So what are you going to do now? Are you going to leave him?"

"Fucking right. Enough is enough," she gulped down the rest of her red wine and then threw the glass at the wall angrily. She put her hands back to her face and began to sob again. "I can't believe he did this shit to me again!"

I looked at Tierra feeling sorry for her. She didn't deserve this. She was a good woman; beautiful, smart, a business woman, a go getter and loyal as fuck. It's always the loyal bitches that get hurt the most. But the scandalous hoe-ass, smut-ass bitches stay getting these loyal ass niggas. Life is so fucked up that way.

Tierra needed to be held so I put my arms around her. She tried to resist me at first but I held her tighter until she gave in. She cried louder and harder as I held her.

"My God, this shit hurts. It's one thing to know. But to see the shit with your own eyes. I saw them in his office tonight fucking. This shit hurts," she sobbed. I shushed her as I rubbed the back of her neck not saying much. Shit, what could I say? I tried to warn her ten years ago and she ain't listen. But now ain't the time for I told you sos.

"Can you make the pain stop?" Tierra asked me softly.

"Make it stop how?" I asked her back. She didn't say anything and I caught on. "That won't make the pain stop forever, Tee. It might help you tonight, but the pain will be right back tomorrow."

"I'm not worried about tomorrow. I just want to get through tonight. I'll worry about tomorrow when it gets here," she said to me. I was silent for a moment. "Please?" she said again.

It wasn't that she was begging me that made my dick hard, just the mere thought of laying with her again like we used to in college turned me on.

We went upstairs to the bedroom and I undressed her slowly. Tonight wasn't the night for fucking. Tonight was the night for me to show this woman one more time how much I loved her. Tonight was my chance to show her that I was a better man for her than Markel was.

I kissed over her bare shoulders, moving her hair to the side so I could kiss her neck. I kissed her slowly and gently as if I were drinking from her mouth, tasting every drop of her. After I got undressed, I laid on the bed with her, kissing her and exploring her body as if it were the first time. She wrapped her arms and legs around me as she breathed heavily against me.

"Please," she said again softly. I knew what she wanted and what she needed and I gave it to her. I made love to her until her body exploded. She trembled underneath me while I held her hands above her head with our fingers intertwined. All I could do was stare at her. She always was and will always be the most beautiful woman in the world to me. I laid next to her and wrapped my arms around her. She snuggled close to me and fell asleep in my arms. I whispered in her ear that I loved her and moments later I fell asleep.

19

Tierra

"So this is what the fuck you do? I know what I did was fucked up. But you wait until I leave and fuck my best friend! In my muthafucking bed?! You tramp-ass bitch, wake the fuck up!" The sound of Markel's very pissed off voice woke me outta my sleep. I was startled and scared at first, until the images of that blonde haired bitch riding his dick in his office popped in my head, reminding me of the fucked up night I had previously. I squinted against the light and rubbed my eyes after easing away from Darnell and sat up. Wait... did this nigga just call me a tramp-ass bitch?

"What the fuck did you just call me?" I asked as I grabbed a t-shirt and put it on quickly.

"Bitch, you heard me," Markel seethed. He moved like lightning towards the bed and I jumped up. But he wasn't coming for me, he was coming after Darnell. Oh shit, it's about to go down. He snatched Darnell out of his sleep, grabbing him by his throat and punched his best friend square in the jaw.

"Markel! Stop it, what the hell are you doing?" I screamed at him. Darnell woke up in defense mode and swung back. He realized it was Markel and looked at him surprised.

"Yo nigga, what the fuck?!" Darnell yelled.

"You're fucking my wife in my bed and you got the nerve to ask me questions?!" Markel was hot. I had never seen him this angry before. Karma's a bitch. Markel swung on Darnell again but he managed to block it. He grabbed Markel by his collar and wrestled him onto the bed. They struggled with each other as I screamed for them to stop though deep inside I was hoping Darnell kicked his fucking ass. Oh Lord, they were both on their feet boxing like they were in the middle of the street, giving each other the business. But somehow, Darnell got Markel in a choke hold and hemmed him up against the wall.

"You've been cheating on Tierra since high-school but you're mad because she flipped the script on you! And you got the balls to swing on me, nigga?!" Darnell practically growled in Markel's face.

Yani

Okay, I had seen enough. I went over to them and tried to separate them. "Okay, y'all stop it! That's enough! Darnell, let him go!" I practically had to pry Darnell's fingers from off of Markel's collar so I could separate them. Darnell let him go with a jerk, pushing Markel into the wall. I stood in between the two of them. I then looked at Markel.

"So this is what you do? Call yourself paying me back. Of all people, did it have to be my best friend?" Markel said to me as he breathed heavily. I could actually see the hurt in his face.

"You mad, or nah?" I said back with the most evil expression on my face. "You got some fucking nerve calling me a tramp-ass bitch after all the whoring you did over the last fifteen years."

"He called you a what?" Darnell said after throwing on his jeans. "Aww nigga, you lame as shit for that one. This your fucking wife, dawg. So the fuck what she paid you back nigga, look how dirty you been doing her all this time. You fucking bitches at the office, lying to her face, lying behind her back. Now you wanna flip a script? Get the fuck outta here with that shit, nigga."

"Yo Darnell, mind your business. This is between me and my wife. You hit it, alright. Whatever. I knew you wouldn't hesitate to get the easy hit if the chance came up so I'm not even gonna trip over it. But trust and believe that shit won't happen again."

That was the third time he disrespected me. "You're calling me easy now?" I shook my head. "Unfucking-believable."

"Darnell, you need to get the fuck outta my house so I can talk to my wife," Markel said to his best friend. Darnell looked at him and then looked at me to see what I was going to say. I nodded my head for him to go.

Darnell threw his shirt and sneakers on and walked past me, grabbing my hand briefly. "Call me if you need to talk," he said to me tenderly.

"Nigga…" Markel said as he made a move towards Darnell as though he was going to swing on him again. I put my hand on his chest to stop him and Darnell left.

Markel stared at me and I stared back at him. The silence in the room was unbearable but I wasn't going to be the first one to say something. He looked me over and then shook his head.

"Why did it have to be Darnell?" he asked me.

"Why did it have to be anybody?" I asked back. The room fell silent again. Shockingly I wasn't angry. I thought the site of my husband would have sent me into a screaming rage again. "Why did you always cheat on me, Markel? How come I was never enough?" I looked him in his eyes as I waited for an answer.

Markel shook his head and shrugged. "I don't know." He looked away unable to give me eye contact.

"Don't give me that bullshit answer. This ain't high-school. Answer me like a man. Answer me like I'm your wife," I demanded. I waited for a moment for him to respond. "Am I ugly?" I asked him.

He looked up at me. "No, don't be ridiculous."

"Are you not attracted to me anymore? Am I not fucking you good enough? Am I boring to you? What is it Markel? Because I have been wracking my brains over the last fifteen years trying to figure out what the fuck is wrong with me that make you flock to these other bitches. In high-school, it was easy. I figured maybe it was because I wasn't giving it to you. As the saying goes, what one woman won't do, there are plenty of other bitches who will do it and more. So I gave you my virginity and that wasn't enough. Not meaning to, I got

231

pregnant. I gave you a child. That still wasn't enough. I stood by your side, took care of home, encouraged you, did everything you asked me to do and that still wasn't enough. I married you and even that wasn't enough. So what is it because I am all out of answers and I am fucking tired?"

Markel was quiet for a moment before he said anything. "With men it's simple. It wasn't a matter of things you weren't doing for me or areas you were lacking in. It was the thrill of not getting caught, I guess."

"So this was a game to you?" I asked as I looked at him with a frown. "How many bitches can I fuck before Tierra catches me? The question should have been how many bitches can I fuck before Tierra finally kills me?! I fucking knew all along!"

"Then how come you never said anything?" Markel asked me. "If you knew I was doing you dirty, how come you never said anything? Because keeping quiet is making me think you didn't care and was off doing your own thing. You jumped in bed real fast with my best friend last night."

"Oh no, don't you dare turn this shit around on me! If you weren't fucking your assistant, last night never would've fucking happened!" I yelled at Markel. He shook his head and sat on the side of our bed. "Do you love her?" I asked him again.

Markel looked up at me. "No, I don't love her. I didn't love her or any of the other chicks. It was just sex. That's it."

I searched Markel's face to see if he was lying but it felt like it was the truth. He stood back up and grabbed my hand.

"We can get through this. I can forgive you for last night. And I know you can forgive me, too. I need you to forgive me. I don't want to lose you or my family…"

I snatched my hand away from him and looked at him with pure contempt. "You should've thought about that a little sooner. It's too late this time, I'm done."

"Tierra, it's never going to happen again, I promise you. I'll go to counseling, we can go to counseling. I'll do whatever you need me to do, whatever you want me to do. Just please don't leave me," Markel begged me. Was that fear or pain that I heard in his voice?

"No Markel. You obviously don't respect me because if you did, you wouldn't have played a game of fucking bitches until you got caught. I'm fucking done."

"Tierra please," Markel said. And then this man got on his knees. "I'm sorry, please. I'm begging you, please give me another chance to make it up to you." I backed away from Markel, looking down at him with a frown. My husband was on his knees begging and pleading for me not to leave him. Wait, were those tears? "I'm sorry babe. I will never cheat on you again. I will never disrespect you again. I will never hurt you again. I love you and the thought of not having you in my life and losing you for good is killing me. I'm begging you Tierra, please."

I was at a loss for words. I closed my eyes and thought of my father and how he was killed, why he was killed. I thought of the pain my mother was in and how much she cried on the nights he didn't come home like he was supposed to. I then thought of my life without Markel. I tried to see myself without Markel and I couldn't. Markel was my life. The difference between me forgiving him then only for him to cheat on me again was there was never a confrontation, just me trying to change for him without seeing what he needed from me in order to make our relationship work. Forgiving him now that he knows that I have known all along and with it being a confrontation gives us the opportunity to work on the weaknesses in our relationship and turn them into strengths. Everything is out in the open now...well... not EVERYTHING but enough... Maybe counseling could help us. But if we try counseling and this nigga does me dirty one more time, I'm not even going to give him the opportunity to beg me not to leave. One day he'll come home and I'll be gone.

I took a deep breath and opened my eyes. I couldn't say anything, all I could do was nod my head. Markel stood up and hugged me tightly.

"Not so fast," I said as I pulled away from him. "I have a few requests. First off, we go to marriage counseling. I promised to love you for better or worse and this is our worse, but I still love you. You promised to honor and obey and now I'm asking you to honor and obey my requests," I said to Markel.

"Whatever you want..."

I shushed Markel because I knew right now he would blow circus bubbles up my ass if he thought that would stop me from leaving him. "This ain't about to be all talk and no action. You want to stay married, show me! No bull-shit talk and half measures. Show me that you honor me. Show me that you love me and that you don't want to lose me and your family. Because if this shit happens again, we're done. You can start by getting rid of that bitch at the office. I want her ass gone. Assign her to your other facility, call the agency and ask that they give her another position. But you better get her the hell outta that office or I'ma beat that bitch's ass," I said to him with a straight face.

"I'll have her assigned to the office in Langhorne. One of my partners needs an assistant," Markel said to me. He wrapped his arms around me and held me tightly. "I swear to you that I never meant to hurt you and I will do whatever it takes to make it up to you and make this right. I love you, Tee."

I hugged him back and buried my face in his chest so I could smell his cologne. "I love you, too." I told him. I then thought of Darnell and let my husband go. "You gotta patch things up with Darnell," I said to him.

Markel shook his head, "Nah. That's one thing I cannot promise to do and I need you to respect that."

"But y'all were best friends before you even met me, Markel. Don't let the bull-shit stop y'all friendship."

"Nah, fuck that. See, maybe you never noticed but I always peeped how he would look at you. I always knew in the back of my head that he had a thing for you. You say you knew things that I didn't know that you knew. Well I knew some things too, and that nigga couldn't wait for some shit to go down with us so he could hit. I bet he called himself swooping in like Captain Save-a…" he trailed off and looked at me seeing the expression on my face to let him know to pick his words carefully. "…Captain Save a Dame trying to comfort and console you, knowing you was upset and vulnerable. So to me, the nigga took advantage. You're my wife. Regardless what happened between me and you, that shit he did was unforgiveable." Markel was heated.

"So you can forgive me, but you can't forgive the man who's been your best friend for over twenty years?" I asked him in disbelief.

"You're my wife. Darnell… I don't know. Maybe later on down the road. But right now, nah fuck that. That was a violation. I need you to respect that."

I nodded my head and then looked around. Who the hell was going to clean this shit up?

As if Markel read my mind, he said to me, "I'll call a cleaning service and have them come in here and take care of everything. You can handle replacing the furniture. I'll leave my credit card."

"Where are you going?" I asked him as I grabbed some things so I could get a shower.

"You told me to get rid of Candice. I need to do the paper work to have her transferred over. I also have patients," Markel said as he took out his mini tablet from his bag and began fiddling with it.

"No, today you are working from home. Have someone reschedule your patients for another day. Our marriage takes priority. And right now, you can start fixing it by getting your ass in the shower with me," I said in my dominant voice. I started walking towards our bathroom and pulled the t-shirt over my head so I was completely naked. And like the puppy dog he was, Markel followed behind me.

19

Darnell

There was a lot of whispering and chit-chatter at the office when I got to work. I didn't think the chatter was about me and Tierra but I was almost positive the chatter was about Candice and Markel. That nigga had a lot of nerve swinging on me like that. He lucky I didn't break his fucking jaw in that house. Homeboys or not, one thing you don't do is take a fucking swing at me. I've seen niggas get killed in the street for less than that. The disrespect is something I don't tolerate.

I stared at Candice for a while as she did her work. She looked like she wasn't worried at all. I wouldn't be surprised if she believed Markel would leave Tierra for her and they would be together. She suddenly struck me as being an arrogant bitch like that.

I had no doubt in my mind that Tierra would leave Markel this time. After last night, I didn't see her taking him back. Since Candice obviously was a slut, I knew she

239

would never be wife material. Maybe Tierra and I would finally have our chance. Maybe I could find out about Tianna, too. Might as well.

Candice looked up and caught me staring at her and then looked back at her computer screen. I felt a need to confront this bitch. I walked over to her and pulled a chair up to her desk.

"Looks like you're the talk of the office," I said in a low voice.

"I don't know what you're talking about," Candice said blandly as she worked.

"Oh… so you're just going to pretend that everybody isn't in here talking about Markel's wife catching you two in his office fucking after everybody left last night?" Candice looked up at me startled and then quickly looked back at her computer monitor.

"It'll blow over. It's just office gossip," she said casually.

"Well at least I know why you didn't have time for me. Too busy fucking and sucking on the boss. Hoes be like…" I snickered as I went back to my desk. Candice looked at me with contempt but what could she say? Skank-ass bitch. Her phone rang and she answered it.

"Yes, Mr. Davis…" I heard her say. "You want me to clear your schedule for the day, sir…? What time will Mr. Bradley be needing me today…? Okay, sir… Yes Mr. Davis… You have a good day as well." Candice disconnected the call and began gathering up some things. She came over to my desk as she put her coat on.

"Mr. Davis is going to be out for the rest of week. His schedule has been cleared for the week. I will be working out of the Langhorne office assisting Mr. Bradley."

"Sending you to Langhorne… look like that's the start of him getting your ass outta here. But don't worry, I hear Bradley is married too, and likes them young." I chuckled to myself and Candice walked away from me. Hoes who take the high road… kind of an oxymoron.

I decided to text Tierra to see how she was doing. I started with a simple "good morning text". She responded moments later saying good morning back. I text her again asking her if she was okay. She replied telling me that she was hanging in there. I offered to pick up dinner for us after work and come over to keep her company and talk. She declined five minutes later stating that she just wanted to be alone and was cleaning up the house but would text me later. I told her to take it easy but let her know I was here if she needed to talk. She responded saying "Ok" with a smiley face. I sent a smiley face back.

I knew she would need time to process the fact that her and Markel were over so I didn't want to pressure her but it was important for her to know that I was here for her. Tierra's a good woman and deserves way better. I just hope that she's smart enough to see it this time. And even if she doesn't choose me, as long as she gets the hell away from Markel and finds someone that really appreciates her, that would do her some good. I preferred she chose me but you know, baby steps and all that good shit.

I wouldn't be surprised if Candice was talking in codes. Last I checked, John already had an assistant so why would he need Candice? Yeah, Markel probably was calling Candice to some hotel to fuck away his misery. I shook my head at the thought. That's my homie and all but man, he fucked up a good thing he had with Tierra over a piece of ass that's a straight up hoe. She's sucking and fucking both of us and he ain't even know.

20

Tierra

Markel and I showered together but I would not allow him to have sex with me. I've noticed that whenever we fight or have a disagreement, afterwards we have sex and then all seems well. Sex was not going to cure this problem. I didn't want him touching me after seeing with my own two eyes how he touches his whores.

As much as I was hurting over catching him red handed, I could only imagine what seeing me in bed sleeping in the arms of his best friend naked had done to his pride and his ego. I didn't feel sorry for him in the slightest but I knew it was a hurt piece. I didn't apologize and wouldn't apologize either. Had he not been fucking his assistant, I wouldn't have been sleeping in Darnell's arms last night and our house wouldn't look like World War III had taken place.

Markel had to negotiate a handsome fee to get a cleaning service out on such short notice. The look on their faces when they saw the condition of the house and the damage I had done was almost hilarious. I excused myself and went into the kitchen, which outside of the children's bedrooms and bathrooms, was the only room I didn't destroy. Markel went out to pick us up some breakfast while I watched over the cleaning crew to make sure all they did was clean. I know how sometimes fingers can get sticky and shit can turn up missing.

I fixed myself a strawberry smoothie when my phone went off. I saw that it was Xavier. I started not to answer but I remembered the stunt his wife pulled the day before and I decided he needed a curse out.

"You have a lot of nerve calling my fucking phone after the shit you pulled yesterday not to mention the shit your wife pulled causing me to get arrested, Mr. I'm not involved at the moment," I hissed into the phone.

"Tierra listen, I didn't lie about being involved," Xavier tried to explain. More lies.

"You are such a fucking liar!" I said to him.

"Yes, I'm married. But we are in the process of getting a divorce. She's not happy about it and still causes problems whenever she sees me with another woman."

"Shockingly, I don't believe you. Nevertheless, I beat her ass yesterday for trying to run me off the road. I don't have time for nobody's drama or crazy fucking spouses."

"I just wanted to apologize to you. I really would like to make it up to you," Xavier said in a charming voice.

I wasn't moved by his charms today, though. "No need to. I told you we're done. Lose my number."

"And if I don't?" Xavier asked me.

"Xavier, you don't want to try the stalker card with me," I warned him.

"Don't act like what we have between us doesn't mean anything, Tierra."

Was he crazy? "Goodbye Xavier," I hung up the phone. He was really tripping. I shook my head and took a sip from my smoothie. My cell phone rang again. I saw that it was Xavier and sucked my teeth. I started to decline his call but figured he would leave a dumb-ass voicemail, so I answered and then hung up. He called back again.

"This nigga done lost his mind," I mumbled under my breath. I remembered a friend of mine telling me

245

about a call blocking app called Mr. Numbers. I downloaded it and set it to pick up and hang up whenever Xavier called. I also blocked his text after he sent a long drawn out text about much he wanted to be with me and how I should leave my husband so we could be together. This fool was nuts. He then started calling me from a private number.

Oh no, this shit was getting out of hand. I set Mr. Numbers to block Private numbers as well. Leave it to me to fuck a psycho nigga.

Markel came in the kitchen behind me and kissed my neck, making me jump.

"Relax babe, it's just me. You good?" he asked me when he saw the worried expression on my face.

I forced a smile. "Yeah… just thinking."

Markel gave me a peck on the lips. "I spoke to your mom. She's going to keep the kids for the rest of the week while we take some time to work on some things."

I looked at Markel with a frown on my face. "You told her?"

"Not specifically. I just said we were having some problems that needed to be worked out and I asked her if she could keep the kids while we started counseling." I started walking away from Markel and he grabbed my arm to stop me.

"I wish you had said something to me first before you blabbed to my mom. And you know Tamia talks too much and will more than likely tell her how I went off in here last night."

"Baby, if you don't want to tell your mom what's going on, I understand. But we need some time together to work things out. Where else were the kids going to go?" Markel replied as he looked me in my eyes. He was right and I knew it. I just didn't want to deal with my mother and all of her endless questions. I nodded my head, giving in when my phone rang. I looked at it on the table and saw it was from a number I wasn't familiar with. It could have been a new client or it could have been Xavier calling from a different number since I blocked his cell phone and private numbers. I stared at the phone not sure if I should answer.

"Aren't you going to get that?" Markel asked me as he pulled our food from the bag.

Not wanting to seem suspicious, I answered the phone. "Tierra Davis' phone," I said in a calm voice.

"Oh now you want to answer. Don't play games with me, Tierra. You really don't want to get on my bad side because I could fuck you up in a way where you don't even see the shit coming," Xavier threatened.

I swallowed past a knot of fear as I glanced at my husband and then cleared my throat. "Yes, this is she. How can I help you, today?"

"Oh, I guess the hubby is nearby. You don't sound so tough now. Why don't you put him on the phone so I can tell him how much of a fucking slut you are?" Xavier was really turning out to be a crazy bastard.

I took a deep breath. "I'm sorry, my schedule is full right now and I'm not taking any new clients. Thank you for considering my company. Have a blessed day."

"Bitch, you better not hang up on me…" Xavier sneered.

I disconnected the call and turned my ringer off. I was trembling inside as I wondered whether or not Xavier was serious about his threat or if he was just angry from being rejected. What did I get myself into?

Yani

"Not taking any more clients right now?" Markel asked me as he passed me my plate of home fries, scrambled cheese eggs, grits and pork bacon. I had lost my appetite.

I felt my phone vibrate in my hand and knew it was Xavier again. I couldn't look at my husband so I shook my head and cleared my throat. "I'm going to take some time off so we can focus on fixing what's been broken," I said softly. My eyes became teary when I felt my phone vibrate again to alert me of a voicemail and then began ringing again.

Markel was about to put a spoonful of grits in his mouth when he saw the tears in my eyes. I guess he thought I was still hurting over what happened the night before. He came over to me and put his arm around me. "I'm sorry, babe. I really, truly am sorry and I promise I'm going to do better. I promise you that."

I nodded my head and sniffed before pulling away from him. I silently walked out of the kitchen and went upstairs to Tamia's room since the cleaning crew was cleaning the hallway. I called Sprint's Customer Service.

"Yes, I need to change my phone number please..."

How was I going to explain changing my number to my husband? I didn't want to change my number because of the multitude of clients I have as well as the press who would want me to make appearances as well as do interviews. But Xavier was about to be a serious problem that I didn't want to have to deal with. Thankfully he didn't know where I lived. That is the importance of never bringing your action home because you never know when they are going to pull some Fatal Attraction type shit.

I got on my laptop to compose an email to my client list making sure that I left Xavier off when I saw he had spammed me with multiple emails. I can't believe how fucking psycho this asshole was turning out to be. I went inside of the C-Panel to my website and created another email account. I then sent out a bulk email to my client list with the new contact information. Afterwards, I destroyed the old email address. I then updated my website, taking the old contact information down. I started to put the new contact information up but then realized if Xavier came back to my website, he could get it. I opted for a simple contact form instead. Crazy son of a bitch. I also pulled his IP address from the emails he sent me and blocked him. I put my hands to my face when I heard a knock at Tamia's door. I jumped up, startled and then opened the door.

Markel was staring at me looking perturbed. "Are you okay?" he asked me.

"Yes, I'm fine. I'm just tired. I was updating my website and noticed someone was spamming me and then someone kept calling and hanging up. I guess I should have listened to you when you told me to get a business phone and not use my cell-phone," I lied and felt slightly horrible. Just a tad.

"Well, you were on TV. Your name is getting out there so of course the crazies are going to come out. So from now on, since you got people playing on your phone and trying to run you off the road, I don't want you going to anymore appointments by yourself. It's time for you to get yourself an assistant as well as a PR Agent so you don't have to do so much by yourself. You're gonna burn yourself out," Markel said to me as we walked downstairs together.

I nodded my head in agreement as I looked around. "Wow, that cleaning crew did an amazing job," I said.

"I know right. Raymour & Flanigan are going to deliver the items you picked out tomorrow. And I looked into some marriage counselors…" Markel trailed off and I looked at him. He was being proactive, which was a good sign that he wanted to make things work.

"Did any of them grab your attention?" I asked him.

"Yeah… this Dr. Percy. And only because she's Black. Can't go wrong with a Sister shrink," Markel said in a joking manner to lighten the mood. My phone went off and I jumped. I looked at it and saw that it was a Facebook message from Darnell wanting to know if everything was okay because he tried calling me and the number was disconnected. I responded telling him someone was playing on the phone and gave him the new number. I then thanked him for being there for me the night before but told him that me and Markel were going to try to work things out and go to counseling. I'm not sure if he liked that tidbit of information because I didn't get a response back from him.

Markel pulled me into his lap and kissed my chin. "We're going to get through this," he said to me.

Yani

"I hope so," I replied. I was still distracted and a little shaken up over what Xavier said and did earlier in the day.

"I know so," Markel replied as he kissed me. I kissed him back, feeling safe in his arms. Yes, my husband fucked up big time. But he was right. As long as we were both willing to put in the work, we could get through this and come out even stronger than before.

21

Markel

I was willing to do whatever I had to do to keep Tierra in my life. It was time for me to grow the fuck up and leave the childish games and adulterous affairs with these bitches in the past. I knew I couldn't outright fire Candice because her work performance had been nothing short of impeccable during her two months at the office. Instead, I had her transferred to our Langhorne office after remembering that John needed a new assistant because the one he had was leaving for a position in New York.

Candice called me while I was out getting breakfast for me and Tierra.

"Yes, Candice?" I answered on the Bluetooth while I was still in the car.

"Mr. Davis, is everything okay with us?" she asked me.

"Yes, everything is fine. I'm just taking some time off from work to take care of some things at home. Our other office in Langhorne is short staffed and John Bradley needs a new assistant. Since I won't be in this week, I didn't want to leave you with nothing to do so you'll be working from that office."

"I don't mean in that regard, sir. I mean between us. Our relationship."

I was silent for a moment, not sure how I should respond. I cleared my throat and said, "Candice, I've enjoyed the time that we spent together and I think you are an incredible woman. If I weren't married, I could easily see you as someone I would want to see on a regular basis. But I am married and this isn't news to you," I explained to her as gently as I possibly could.

"But if you were happily married, you would not have been spending so much time with me," she replied.

"No marriage is perfect, I admit that. But she is my wife and I love her." I was so hoping I didn't have to go through the motions with this chick.

"So you're not leaving your wife...?" she asked me. No way did she seriously think I was going to leave my wife for her.

"No Candice, I am not leaving Tierra."

"What about me? What about all of the passion between us? What about all of the times we've shared? Are you saying that it meant nothing to you… that I meant nothing to you?" Candice's voice sounded as though she was going to cry. Oh boy, here we go.

"Candice, it was just sex. We talked about this when it first started. Just sex, nothing more. It's not like you didn't know I was married."

"How could you do this to me?" I fell silent not knowing what else to say to her. I hate when side chicks try to switch lanes and become the main chick. "I'm not letting you just toss me to the side like I'm some piece of trash you're discarding," she replied, now sounding as though she was getting angry.

"You're not letting me? Candice, let me explain something to you. This is how the game is played. You fucked a married man; understand the chances of that married man leaving his wife for you are slim to none. So for future reference, if you want to avoid getting your pretty little feelings hurt, try fucking a single man that intends to do more than just fuck you or have you suck his dick. We are finished. Have a good day at work." I disconnected the call becoming quickly annoyed. See how bitches switch up on you the minute you stop supplying them with good dick? She sent me a text message saying:

'I hate you, you black bastard! You're not going to get away with this. I will make your life a living hell!'

"Try it, bitch," I mumbled to myself. She didn't want me to unleash Tierra on that ass. I grabbed the breakfast for me and Tierra and made my way back home.

We had a great night that evening. The house was quiet. We both soaked in the hot tub letting the bubbles sooth us. We sipped champagne as we talked over our plans to make our marriage work and get pass each other's affairs. I could tell that Tierra wasn't ready for me to touch her yet so I opted to hold her in my arms. Fuck it, I'd just beat off in the shower or when she goes to sleep... seriously.

I had never gotten around to my little jack-off session since I fell asleep. Tierra nudged me, waking me up.

"Markel, wake up," she said to me as she pushed on my shoulder.

257

"Yeah baby, what's wrong?" I asked in a sleepy voice.

"I think I just heard something downstairs or out front," Tierra replied. I lay in the bed wondering what Tierra was talking about and listened. I didn't hear anything.

"I don't hear anything, babe. Go back to sleep," I told her as I put my arms back around her.

"I'm telling you, I heard something," Tierra insisted.

I huffed and sat up in the bed and listened again. I heard a trash can fall over and flinched. "It's probably just a raccoon digging in the trash. I'll clean it up in the morning…" Just as the words fell from my lips we heard a crash as if a window was breaking. Tierra screamed and I threw my hand over her mouth. We heard another crash and then the sound of Tierra's Range Rover alarm going off.

"What the fuck?" she mumbled from behind my hand.

"Stay right here," I replied as I eased from the bed. Did someone just bust the windows out of my baby's car? I crept down the stairs and just as I suspected, Tierra was right behind me. I couldn't blame her after what

258

we'd just heard. I crept over to the window in the foyer and looked out. "Oh shit…" I said aloud.

"What?!" Tierra asked as she came behind me and peeked out of the window too. When she saw it, she went off.

"Who the fuck… No the fuck… Hold the fuck on!!!" she snapped as she unlocked the door and turned the light to the driveway on.

Someone took a brick and smashed her windshield as well as the back window and the driver side window. They carved "Hoe Ass Bitch" in the side of her truck and emptied the trash can filled with garbage on the truck. They also flattened all four of her tires. Tierra looked at her truck in horror. I had silenced the alarm as I circled the truck to see the damage. I then looked down both ends of the driveway to see if I saw anyone fleeing the scene.

Neither one of us knew what to say as we both looked at her truck with our mouths gaped open. My car hadn't been touch which led me to believe whoever tried to run her off the road, came back for more payback. Now I was wondering was her relationship with this Jenkins character strictly business after all? I also thought maybe it was Candice. But she was more likely to smash out my windows than Tierra. I didn't rule her out completely. But I was more so leaning towards the road rage chick.

Tierra's eyes were cold and filled with rage when she looked at me. I was expecting her to start screaming, but instead she stormed in the house. I followed her inside and grabbed the house phone. It was 1 o' clock in the morning. AAA would come get the truck but there was no-where to take it. Our mechanic definitely wasn't open at this hour. I could hear Tierra chipping away at ice in the kitchen. Yeah, a drink was definitely needed right about now.

Instead of calling AAA, I called the police to file a police report. While we were waiting for them, I went to one of the closets and got one of our large, King sized blankets, and threw it over the truck. Didn't need the nosey-ass neighbors taking pictures and posting the shit on Instagram. That's not the kind of publicity my wife needed. I went in the kitchen and rubbed the back of her neck as she sipped her drink.

"If that bitch from your office did this shit, I swear no amount of reasoning will keep me from beating her fucking ass," Tierra said maliciously.

"Calm down, babe. I honestly don't think it was her," I replied.

"Ooooh Markel, you do not want to take her side with the way I'm feeling right now. Seriously." Tierra gulped down her drink and poured herself some more.

"Baby, I'm not taking her side, trust me. If it's proven that she did this, I wouldn't even stop you. But don't you think if it were her she would have fucked my shit up and not yours? Why would she carve *hoe ass bitch* in your truck instead of my car?" Tierra fell silent as if she was thinking over what I said. She then shook her head.

"Who knows? Maybe she didn't touch yours because it would look too obvious," she replied.

"True," I agreed. I then chuckled to lighten the mood. "Maybe it was Darnell." Tierra spit her drink out and we started laughing.

"Shut up! It wasn't no damn Darnell. His lazy ass would never drive up here just to fuck up my car. I think it was your assistant."

261

"I think it was the road rage bitch," I replied.

Tierra hesitated for a moment and then shook her head. "Nah, she doesn't know where I live. And that was already straightened out."

"Whoever it was, they were outta fucking pocket for that shit." I kissed her neck when I heard the doorbell ring. Glad to see the officers didn't take all day.

We answered their questions and I gave them Candice's information. Tierra gave them as much information as she could remember from the incident in Delaware and the police took photos of Tierra's car. An hour after they arrived, they were leaving. I covered the truck again and we went inside, locked up and turned on the alarm. Tierra was already upstairs lying in the bed. She looked like she was in deep thought when I joined her.

"I'll have AAA pick the truck up first thing in the morning and send it over to the mechanic. It's gonna be a couple weeks until it's fixed. Insurance is going to be crazy. Good thing we have coverage for vandalism,"

"Yeah," Tierra replied as she stared blankly at the ceiling. I wondered what she was thinking at the moment and couldn't help feeling guilty over what happened.

Yani

What if her truck was mangled because of the affair I was having with Candice? Something in me told me that what happened to her car wasn't because of something I did but because of something she had done.

I kissed her ear and sucked on her ear lobe for a moment before I said what was on my mind. "Baby, look at me." Tierra turned and faced me, giving me her undivided attention. "The only way this marriage counseling is going to work for us is if there aren't any secrets between us. Are you sure there isn't anything that you want to tell me?"

Tierra shook her head as she looked me in my eyes. "I don't have anything else I want to tell you, Markel."

I searched her face for a moment and then kissed her. I pulled her on top of me and kissed her longingly as I ran my fingers through her hair. "I want to make love to my wife tonight," I said to her as I kissed her neck.

"I want to make love to my husband tonight," she said back with a giggled.

"Ugh, thank God. I thought you put me on pussy punishment," I said as I pulled her shirt over her head. She laughed as I kissed her. It felt good to touch my wife again. I squeezed her large breasts gently in my hands and rolled my thumb over her nipples knowing that turned her on. "The kids aren't here. You can scream as loud as you want," I told her as she eased out of her panties. She kissed down my neck and over my chest as she helped me out of my sweat pants. She came back up and kissed me again.

"Make me," she said with a seductive grin on her face. I was definitely up for the challenge. Before the night was over, the neighbors knew my name, my nickname and some extra freaky shit that my wife screamed out during our session. And we ended it as we normally do, facing each other with the lights on. This woman was amazing. I was never going to let another woman come between us again.

22

Tierra

I couldn't believe someone bust the windows outta my car on some Jazmine Sullivan shit! Something in me believed it was Markel's assistant, but after the stunt Xavier pulled earlier, I wouldn't be surprised if it was his punk-ass. But if it was him, how the fuck did he find me?

After the mind blowing sex my husband and I had, I couldn't seem to fall asleep. I was on edge as I pondered over who could have possible tore up my car. A long time ago, I wanted to get my license to carry. Markel was totally against it, saying he didn't like the idea of guns being in the house with the kids. It was time to rethink that shit now, though.

The next morning, Markel had the truck towed to our mechanic and went along to speak with him about the damages. My mother called me on my cell phone.

"Hi Mommy," I replied as I sat eating a BLT.

"Hi sweetie, how are you?" my mother asked back.

"I'm doing okay." I knew why my mother was really calling. Having Markel ask her to keep the kids for a week and more than likely Tamia told her about my "episode" the other night, she was probably a little curious about what was going on with us.

"What are you doing today? Are you working?" she asked me.

"No. I'm taking some time off. I need a break."

"Uh huh," she said casually. Oh boy, here it comes. "How come you changed your cell number?"

I hesitated for a moment. "I was getting prank calls. Probably someone who saw me on TV and was being a jerk. So I'm not going to place my new number on my website or my business cards until I get an actual office." I explained.

"Uh huh," she said again. I rolled my eyes. "Markel told me you two are going to counseling."

"Yes we are, Mom."

"I gather he's still cheating on you," she naturally assumed.

"No marriage is perfect, Ma. We just want to make sure ours stay strong and lasts long."

266

Yani

My mother snorted as if what I said was a joke. After what my father had done to her, she had become bitter. Her philosophy was- once a cheater, always a cheater. And I could understand why she felt that way. But all men weren't like that. Anything worth fighting for is worth having and my marriage was worth fighting for.

"Come on by the house so we can talk," she said to me.

"We're on the phone, why can't we just talk now?" I asked.

"Excuse me?" my mother replied as if what I said was disrespectful.

"I can't right now. My truck is in the shop and Markel is out with the other car. I'll have to wait until he comes back," I explained, hoping she would drop it.

"All that money you have, why don't you just rent another car?"

"Mom…" I groaned.

"When Markel comes back home, come by the house so we can talk. Y'all done dumped these kids on me, the least you can do is stop by."

"Mom, nobody dumped my kids on you. Markel asked and you said it was okay," I snapped. I hate when she talks like this.

"Who do you think you're talking to like that?" she asked back.

"You always do that, Ma. If my kids are a problem, I can come get them so you don't have to worry about them being dumped on you."

"You better watch your tone, young lady. Tamia told me about your little tantrum you threw over there. Don't think you're going to pull one of your tantrums on me." I let out a sigh and shook my head. Tamia talks too damn much. "When Markel comes home, make tracks to my house. And don't make me come up there, ya understand?" my mother said to me.

"Yes ma'am." She kissed in my ear and we disconnected the call.

I was not in the mood for my mom's shit today. I just caught my husband cheating, I had a psycho stalker on my ass and to top it off, somebody fucked up my car. I love my mom to death, but if she started her shit today, I swear I'm finna tell her something the good Lord will just have to forgive me for later… seriously.

Markel came in and gave me a brief kiss but he had a long face.

"Babe, what's wrong?" I asked him.

Markel shook his head, "The damage to your truck was too severe. They didn't just bust out windows and scratch it up and slash your tires. They poured anti-freeze in your gas tank and it fucked up the engine. So the insurance company is marking it as totaled."

I shook my head in anger. If I ever find out who fucked my shit up, I was going to give them the Guinness book of records ass whipping, trust.

"Bitch," I mumbled.

"I know, babe. So what we can do is head over to the dealership and grab something this weekend and just rock out with the Acura until Saturday," Markel replied.

"Yeah, that'll work." I took a deep breath to shake off my annoyance. If I were going to visit my mother, I needed to go with a pleasant attitude at least. Whatever my attitude is after that will depend on her behavior. "Mom wants to see me so do you have anywhere to go?" I asked Markel.

"I have to stop at the office for a few things and that's about it. You want me to drop you off and then pick you up afterwards?" he asked in return.

Not having a car fucking sucked already. I hate being at the mercy of anyone needing a ride. "Yeah, that's fine. I'll just call when I'm ready to go."

Markel drove me over to my mother's house. He knew better than to pull some double park, drop off shit. He came inside to speak to her before leaving.

"How are you, Markel?" My mother asked pleasantly. "I wasn't expecting you."

"I'm just dropping Tierra off before I head over to the office and take care of some things," Markel said with a smile.

My mother looked at him suspiciously as if she didn't believe him. She then fixed her eyes on me. "What exactly happened to your car, Tierra?"

"It was vandalized," I said blandly. She looked at me with a raised eyebrow. I could just imagine what she was thinking.

"Call me when you're ready, okay?" Markel said before giving me a kiss. I nodded my head. "Nice seeing you Mrs. Andrews."

Yani

"Encantada," my mother said with a smirk. I rolled my eyes and went to sit in her dining room as Markel left.

"Tamia tells me that you had some kind of a temper tantrum in the house the other night and started smashing things. And now Markel wants me to keep the kids so the two of you can go to counseling. Has he gone back to his adulterous ways?"

"Mom, I really don't want to talk about it," I said as I sat in a chair.

"When I was your age and your father was running around doing the things that he was doing, my mother tried talking to me and I said the same thing; I really don't want to talk about it. You don't know how many nights I wished that I had my mother to talk about things to after she died," My mother said as she disappeared into the kitchen. She returned moments later with a tray carrying a tea kettle and teacups. Mmm… peppermint tea. She used to fix this for me after my father died and I would sip it as she brushed my hair and we listened to Earth Wind and Fire. A splash of honey and two sugars. I smiled when I heard the familiar clanking noise the spoon made against the teacup as I stirred the tea, giggling like I was twelve again as my mother softly blew in her teacup and the steam fogged up her glasses.

"Talk to me, sweetheart. What is going on between you and Markel? Is he cheating again?" my mother asked me.

I blew into my hot tea and took a tiny sip as I thought over how I could answer her. "Yes, Ma. He cheated again. But we've talked and decided that we are going to try marriage counseling and try to work through this."

"Don't be stupid, Tierra. God, he's been doing this to you since you were fifteen years old. Is your self-esteem that low that you'll allow a man to continuously disrespect you and lay with him every night while turning the other cheek, just to say you have man? What is it going to take before you realize he just isn't the man for you?"

I looked at my mother over my teacup and sat it down on the dining room table. I stared at her for a moment before saying anything. "How low was your self-esteem, Momma?"

"Excuse me?" my mother replied as she looked at me with a frown.

272

"I wish I could. How low was your self-esteem?" I asked her again. "How desperate were you to hold onto Daddy that all you did was sit at the table crying at night instead of calling him on his shit? Because I don't remember you being so courageous back then. What was with you that you continuously laid with my father at night knowing that he was out whoring while you sat at home crying your eyes out?"

Right after the words fell from my mouth, my mother back slapped me in it. Reflex brought my hand to my face where she hit me and I scooted back in fear that she would hit me again. My eyes instantly became teary.

"How dare you?" my mother asked me as her eyes became teary as well. "Unlike you, I didn't have a career and money to fall back on where I could just up and leave him and live well. Or have you forgotten how we struggled after he was killed?! Unlike you, I didn't have a mother or family support to fall back on if I did conjure up the courage to leave him. So for the sake of you and making sure you didn't go without and making sure your upbringing was as normal as I could make it, I stayed. I endured and yes it was hell. But I didn't endure because I had some bullshit idea that he would change and we would live happily ever after. I stayed out of necessity. And what the hell did it get me? What the hell did it get us? Not one damn thing except a lesson poorly learned with history repeating itself through you." My mother wiped her eyes and we fell silent.

"I'm not staying with Markel out of necessity, Momma. I'm staying because I love him. I love him," I said after a moment, becoming choked up.

My mother snickered as she stared at me as though I was the dumbest woman in the world. "What's love got to do with it?"

"A lot, Momma. A lot. You never confronted Daddy. You say you endured for me? No, you endured because you were a coward. Maybe I am stupid for believing that love is enough to make Markel commit to me. But that is for me to decide, not you!" I stood up and snatched my purse from the table. I knew coming here was going to piss me off. It never fails.

"Tierra Regine!" my mother called to me. It had been awhile since I heard her call me by my first and middle name. I stopped with my back facing her. She stood behind me and when I turned around, she hugged me. That was something she hadn't done since my father was killed. "I'm sorry," she apologized. "I was wrong for slapping you and calling you stupid. Please sit and finish your tea with me."

I nodded my head and sat back down with my mother. We talked for another hour about my catering business and other things. I didn't tell her the details of how I caught Markel cheating nor did I tell her about Xavier or Darnell. But I did sit down and chant Daimoko with my mother and did Gongyo with her as well. The one thing about Buddhism that remained constant with me is that it brought me peace. I felt much better... until Markel came to get me and I saw that he had been in a fight. What the hell, man...?

23

Markel

I needed to run to the office to grab a few things so I could handle the desk work from home. I wasn't surprised at some of the dirty stares I received from a few of the female workers. Look at me sideways if you want to. Just remember who writes the got damn checks. Yes, humble yourselves. I knew those broads weren't mad that I committed adultery. They were mad that the adultery wasn't committed with them. Yeah, females are just sickening that way.

This was supposed to just be a stop, cop and bop so I could go pick my wife up and we could do our first marriage counseling session. Man, nothing ever goes smoothly or according to plan.

As I was at my desk briefly checking emails while I transferred a few files over and was gathering some paperwork, Darnell stood in my doorway.

Yani

"How can I help you today?" I said, trying to be professional even though a part of me wanted to steal the shit outta him again for running up in my wife.

"I was under the impression you wouldn't be back until next week," Darnell said.

"I'm not back just yet. I'm just grabbing a few things and then I'm leaving. Did you need something?" I asked, barely looking up from my desk.

"I just wanted to give you this." Darnell came into my office and sat a piece of paper on my desk. "I was going to give it to you next week when you came back but since you're here today, there's no time like the present."

I picked up the paper that Darnell gave me and saw it was a letter of resignation. I almost felt bad. This had been my boy since we were five years old. We had seen each other through some good times and extremely bad times, but nothing ever broke up our friendship. I thought about what my wife said and decided that I would forgive him one day. Our friendship may never be the same but, I would forgive him one day.

"I'm sorry to see you go, Darnell. You've been a great employee over the last three years. We'll be happy to give you a letter of recommendation if one is needed or if you ever decide you would like to come back…"

Darnell interrupted me. "That won't be necessary." He left my office and went back to his desk to finish his work quietly. Damn… I was losing one of the only real homies I had in my life. All over some shit that could have been avoided if I wasn't running around behind Candice. I grabbed the things I needed and left the office without saying anything else to Darnell or the other employees. It was when I got out to the parking garage to get in my car that the shit got real.

Candice got out of her car when she saw me. "Markel, we need to talk."

I looked at her and sighed, trying not to become annoyed with her. "Candice, shouldn't you be at the Langhorne office with John?"

"I had to run some errands for him near this office and was on my way up to get some things from my desk when I saw your car and figured I would wait to talk to you." She stood in front of me and I was shocked that nothing about her appearance turned me on as it usually did. I still thought that she was a beautiful woman. But I was not going to risk losing Tierra by messing around

278

with her again. We were silent for a moment as she stood close to me. "I've missed you," she said to me softly.

"Candice…" I started to say.

She stepped closer to me and placed her hand on my chest as she gazed in my eyes. As appealing as her grayish blue eyes were, she still had no effect on me.

"Can you honestly say that you haven't missed me, Mr. Davis; that you haven't missed our nights together? Can you?" she leaned in to kiss me and I grabbed her. She gasped and smiled. I guess she thought this was about to be one of those moments where we had hot, steamy sex in my car. Nah baby. Not today.

"Yes, I can honestly say I haven't missed that," I replied as I moved her away from me.

"Markel, please! What did I do to offend you? What can I do to make it up to you?" she begged me. Was she serious?

"Candice, it's not you. I explained it to you already and I'm not explaining it to you again. I'm not leaving my wife for you. We are never going to be together. Now get the hell away from my car," I said to her. She was doing too much at this present moment and time.

Then Candice did something that I've only allowed my wife to get away with. That bitch put her hands on me. She slapped me in my face and then she spat at me. Ole girl was about to make me lose my religion.

I looked at her with fire in my eyes and she took a step back. "Bitch, you about to seriously get yourself fucked up out here," I practically growled at her.

"I can't believe you'd do this to me! I love you!" Candice cried.

Fuck this, I'm out. I waved her off and tweaked the alarm to my car when I heard a very angry male's voice approaching us.

"Candice!" the man shouted. "What the hell are you doing? I thought your mother was making up lies just to get me to pay closer attention to you. But to hear with my own ears and see with my own eyes, you professing your love to some no good nigger!"

I'm guessing that was her father. The "N" word just granted him a certified ass whipping. But before I could get my hands onto him, he hauled off and slapped the shit outta Candice. She fell into my car and slid to the ground. I was so astounded by his quickness that I didn't move fast enough to intervene. He cocked his fist back as she tried to scurry away and punched her in her shoulder blade, making her cry out.

"Daddy, please! Don't!" she begged as she tried to scoot away from him to get to her feet. He grabbed her by her blonde hair and slapped her again.

"I raised you better than to mingle with got damn mongrels! I've told you before, you lay down with dog's you come up with fucking flees. I send you to the States for you to make an honest career and you're nothing but a nigger-loving whore!" He stood over top of her slapping her as he scolded her like a puppy who had just pissed on the carpet. He had called me a nigger one too many times.

I walked behind him and snatched him by the back of his collar. I spun him around to face me and hit him with a smooth ass Mike Tyson punch knocking him back a step. "Pussy! You got issues with niggas? Well this nigga about to whip ya ass today. You like hitting women? Take this shit!" I said to him as I hit him with a left and a right. Candice screamed for us to stop but I wasn't trying to hear that shit. She ought to be glad I pulled the old man off of her because he looked as though he was going to beat her ass to death.

He blocked one of my punches and managed to sneak his own punch in, catching me across my left jaw. I will admit, he hit hard for an older man. But fuck that, I hit harder. Before I knew it, I had busted his nose and his lip and he was on the ground where his daughter was by the time security came over.

"Coward-ass, bitch! You smacked your daughter around, hit a man!" I said as I towered over him. Security pulled me back and helped Candice's father up off the ground.

"What the hell is going on here?" one of the security guards asked as they stood in between the two of us.

"He attacked my father!" Candice yelled, lying her ass off. I just saved this bitch and she was trying to throw me under the bus. I shook my head in disgust.

"My name is Markel Davis. I work here. He provoked me as well as assaulted her. Don't believe me, check the security tapes. He's on my damn turf pissed off that his precious daughter has a thing for Black men."

One of the security guards was familiar with who I was and had seen me with Candice a few times. He helped her father up off the ground.

Yani

"Do you want to press charges, Mr. Davis?" the guard asked me.

"I might. But I need to go pick my wife up," I turned to Candice, furious at how she flipped the script. Just by that little move she pulled let me know if I had considered leaving my wife for her, this is the kind of shit I would have had to endure with her father and possibly her mother being two racist assholes in 2014. The grass ain't always greener on the other side.

"As for you Ms. Alexander, you have seven days to hand in your letter of resignation, or I will fire you."

She looked at me with wide eyes as if she couldn't believe me. "I could sue you for sexual harassment. You have no idea who you are dealing with." She tried to threaten me. Little bitch.

"And you have no idea who you're fucking with. How would your father's colleagues feel seeing that video of him beating your ass only to get his ass whipped by a nigga? Huh? How would any future employers feel knowing you're a fucking slut that sleeps with her boss to get ahead and then assaults him when she can't have her way? Or did you forget about the little video we made of you sucking my dick in the office before I bent you over

283

my desk? Ruin my life? Bitch, I can make this look too fucking good for reality TV. When I'm done with you, you wouldn't even be able to get a job phone fucking for pennies. And your father will be sweeping and mopping floors for a living. Do you really want to try me?" I said as I stood close to her and talked in a low tone. Candice's eyes swelled up with tears and then she turned towards her father so they could leave. Crazy bitch. I touched the side of my face that her father hit me in and shook my head. Though he only got in that one punch, that was a good punch. I looked at myself in my vanity mirror and saw the bruise that his punch left. Muthafucka. I shook my head. I wasn't even going to cook up a lie to tell my wife. I was just going to give it to her straight. Fuck it; a lie would only make it worse. Now I really was wondering if Candice was the one who bust the windows out of Tierra's car.

The look on Tierra's face when she saw mine was priceless. She leaned back so she could get a better look at me and then shook her head.

"Please tell me you and Darnell didn't get into another fight?" she asked me.

"No, actually we were cool. He handed in his letter of resignation," I told my wife.

Tierra's mouth gaped open. "Did you stop him?" she asked me.

"No, why would I? If he wants to resign over this petty shit, oh well. I'm not about to lose no sleep over this let alone money." I noticed Tierra's mother was watching and listening to us. I forced a smile and waved. "How you doing, Mrs. Andrews."

"Hello again, Markel. Is everything okay?" she asked me.

"Yes, everything is fine," I replied. She looked me over as if she didn't believe me and then looked at Tierra.

"Mom, we have to go. When the kids get here, let them know we will call them tonight when we come from our session," Tierra said before kissing her mother on the cheek.

"Sure sweetie. Call me and let me know how everything went."

"I will, Momma." Tierra and I got inside of my Acura and made our way over to our marriage counselor's office.

"So you wanna tell me who tried to use your face as a punching bag?" Tierra asked me.

I let out a deep sigh and told Tierra what happened in the parking garage to my job as well as how Candice threatened to file a sexual harassment suit against me. "Oh, and the little slut had the nerve to slap me AND spit on me."

"Oh no she didn't! Don't she know where we come from, that's grounds for a bitch to get cut?" Tierra said loudly. "If I were there I would've given her the fucking business, putting her hands on my husband and then having the fucking nerve to spit on him."

"I guess that's what happens when you take good dick away from a psycho bitch," I said and then regretted saying that out loud. Tierra smacked me on my arm.

"Markel, don't get comfortable. Just because we're cordial with each other doesn't mean you can come out your face and say some shit like that and I'll be okay with it. I'm still pissed and none of this shit would be happening if you would've kept your dick in your pants!"

I fell silent knowing Tierra was right. What I said was completely out of line.

Yani

We went through our counseling session which went very well. We talked openly about what was going on with the two of us and what we both wanted out of the sessions as well as how much work we were willing to put in to make out marriage work.

I noticed that Tierra's phone kept going off while we were in counseling. The look on her face when she checked the screen told me that something was wrong that she wasn't speaking on. She suddenly became uneasy and was distracted by whoever that was who called her. Something was going on with her that she wasn't speaking on. Whatever it was had me a little curious. What kind of secrets was she hiding?

24

Tierra

Markel and I had been going to marriage counseling for about a month. We spoke on the concerns that we had in our marriage and brainstormed together on what we could do to make our marriage stronger and better and after trying those things out, our marriage was better than it ever had been. We set nights aside where just the two of us had a date and we also set nights aside where we spent quality time with the kids. Finally things were starting to feel like they should.

It was a shame that Darnell and Markel hadn't patched up their friendship and I felt partially responsible. Markel said he hadn't heard from Darnell since the day he handed in his letter of resignation. When Markel came back to work that Monday, Darnell's desk was cleared and he was gone. He also deleted both of us from his Facebook and was no longer texting me.

Winter was slowly turning into spring and I was getting numerous clients for weddings, graduation parties, retirement parties and other galas. This time of the year is normally my busiest season. But I still made sure I made time for Markel and the kids.

I had my new whip too. With the large commission check Markel got from the commercial Nike did in his Gym along with the money I made from my appearance on the Rachel Ray's Morning Show among other events I catered, I went on and bought a 2013 Mercedes-Benz GL-Class SUV. Where whoever that was thought they would fuck me up by ruining my truck, all they did was put me in the position for something greater.

I finally got a personal assistant like Markel suggested as well as rented office space outside of Mt Airy near Chestnut Hill. I had an unintended late night on a Tuesday for a huge retirement party I was doing for a Fire Fighter. Not only was I doing catering now, but I was also doing event planning and had spent the last three hours with my assistant going over theme settings for this party. We were both exhausted and I decided to send her home ahead of me since it was already after 9pm.

I called Markel from the truck to let him know I was on my way, I just needed to stop at the ATM to pull some money out. I was standing at the ATM doing my transaction when it happened. I don't know why I let my guard down and wasn't paying attention to my surroundings. But as I was putting my card inside of the Wells Fargo ATM machine, I felt a strong hand go over my mouth. I squealed and immediately went into defense mode, swinging my arms and twisted my body so I could get away. I felt whoever it was trying to drag me backwards as if they were trying to take me somewhere. I was almost out of his grasp when he grabbed me by my throat and threw me to the ground. I hit my head and felt dizzy but fought off the blackout that was trying to take me over. My vision was blurry and I couldn't see my attacker fully when they stood over me so I began screaming as loud as I could.

"Hey, what's going on over there?" I heard a loud male voice yell out.

"I'll see you again, bitch," my attacker said, with his voice distorted as though something was over his face. He backed away from me and took off running as another man was approaching me to help.

Yani

"Lady, are you okay?" the man asked me as he knelt in front of me and attempted to help me up.

I was unable to say anything after quickly coming down with a banging headache from being thrown to the ground. Somebody really had the fucking audacity to attack me! I was willing to bet my fucking life that it was Xavier with his crazy ass.

I leaned forward and put my hand to my head, wincing in pain. The world swam around me and I closed my eyes, hoping to fight off the nausea. I hoped I didn't have a concussion.

"Are you okay?" the man asked me again.

"My cell phone is in my pocket. Can you get it for me?" I asked softly.

The man reached in my leather jacket pocket and pulled my iPhone out. I dialed Markel and waited for him to answer.

"Hey Tee, you're running kinda late, is everything okay?" he asked after answering on the second ring.

"I was just attacked," I said. Oh fuck... I needed to vomit. I leaned over and hurled onto the side walk. The man who was kind enough to help me, took the phone from me.

"Hello, my name is Charles. Are you this woman's husband or boyfriend?"

Vomiting always gives me a bad feeling and I began to sob. I wasn't sure if I was angry because I vomited or angry because that bastard had the balls to attack me.

"I'm her husband. Who are you?" Markel asked.

"Your wife was just attacked. I was coming from the store and some guy was trying to rough her up. He threw her onto the ground and I think she may have hit her head." The man named Charles explained. He then gave Markel the location and said he would call the police and sit with me until they arrived.

Charles knelt in front of me again, reaching inside of the plastic bag he had from the store. "Here, I just bought some bottled water. Drink this," he said to me as he twisted the lid off and handed it to me. I took the bottle with a shaky hand and sipped the water gratefully. My head was throbbing. I put the cold bottle against my head, hoping it would make me feel better all the while still pondering over who would want to hurt me.

The cops arrived and moments later, Markel was right behind them. They asked me numerous questions and Charles gave as much information as he could based off of what he saw. Markel shook his hand, thanking him for helping me out and then we rode to the hospital to get me checked out. After my test results came back and it was determined that I had a slight concussion, I truly wanted to kick that muthafucka's ass.

Markel sat beside me on the bed and ran his fingers through my hair. "Babe, what the hell happened tonight?" he asked me.

I shook my head as I looked at the floor. "I honestly have no idea. I went to the ATM to pull some money out because I remembered I needed to pay for Tianna's trip and the next thing I know, some guy grabs me from behind and puts his hand over my mouth so I couldn't scream. I fought back and almost got away from him, but he grabbed me by my throat and threw me to the ground. I hit my head and he stood over top of me as if he were about to do something to me, but then the guy yelled at him and he ran away," I explained to my husband.

Markel took a deep breath and pulled me close to him. "People are getting crazy. These niggas got no picks. Did he say anything to you?"

I thought for a moment, my memory foggy from hitting my head. "He said: I'll see you again, bitch; and then he ran off."

Markel fell quiet and didn't say anything else. The doctors came in and gave me a prescription and advised me to follow up with my primary doctor after giving me the typical advice of coming back if I began vomiting profusely, have any dizzy spells, loss of memory, if I faint or blah blah blah. I just wanted my discharge papers so I could go the hell home. They discharged me and Markel took me home. He called AAA and had them tow my Benz to the house.

After reassuring the kids that I was okay and having them cover me in kisses, Markel saw to it that they all went to bed before coming back to bed with me.

"Tee, look at me," Markel said to me as I was resting on his chest. I looked up at him and he searched my face. "What's going on?" he asked me.

"What do you mean?" I asked in return.

"It's been a lot of weird things happening to you. You had the psycho bitch try to run you off the road, someone vandalized your car and now you have guys attacking you on the street and telling you they're going to see you again as if they know who you are and have some type of beef with you. You have something you want to tell me?" I bit my bottom lip and looked away. A part of me wanted to tell Markel about Xavier but I didn't want him to know that I had cheated on him outside of Darnell. I thought over what I was going to tell him before I opened my mouth. Markel waited patiently for my response.

"I think I have a stalker," I said to him honestly. It wasn't a total lie but it wasn't the complete truth either.

"What do you mean? And how come you never said anything before?" Markel asked as he sat up in our bed and looked at me.

"Well… after I did the Rachel Ray show, remember when I had to change my phone number and make some adjustments to my website? Someone was sending me fan mail. Excessive fan mail. But it wasn't like they were impressed with my work and was just hell bent on meeting me. This was like…" I trailed off for a moment.

"Like they wanted to get inside of your pants," Markel finished for me. I nodded my head without saying anything. "Did they make contact with you after that?"

I nodded my head again. "They started sending me letters to my PO Box saying they were watching me. I thought it was a bunch of BS but then they sent a picture of me as I was coming from the coffee shop on my way to the office."

"Wait a damn minute, Tee. You mean to tell me that someone has been following you, stalking you even, but you wouldn't tell me? And I'm your husband! What the hell happened to us not keeping secrets from each other? What was all that talk about us being open and honest with each other so we could make this marriage work?" Markel ranted. I could tell he was upset and he had a right to be.

"I didn't want to worry you!" I replied back. "Everything was going so good between us, I didn't want to worry you."

"You could have been killed tonight, you understand? You could've been killed."

"But I wasn't," I said softly.

Markel shook his head as he looked at me. "You should've told the cop. The fact that he told you he'll see you again shows that he means business. Until we get this sorted out, you work from home. And don't debate me, Tierra," my husband said sternly. I love it when he's so forceful. I nodded my head in submission and he pulled me close to him. "If I ever find out who's doing this shit, I swear to God."

I snuggled close to my husband and closed my eyes. I should've said something to Markel sooner about the calls and the mail and the photo. To be honest, I was scared as hell. I wasn't sure what Xavier was capable of and that's what made all of this even more scary.

24

Markel

My wife has a stalker. My wife has a fucking stalker and the bastard had the nerve to be following her and even had the balls to not only approach her, but attack her as well. And to make matters worse, she didn't tell me! I know I'm not one to talk about keeping secrets and the damage they can cause considering I kept secrets from her for years, but we agreed that we wouldn't keep secrets from each other anymore.

I went back to the office to get my work done. I had finally found the male assistant that I requested but he wasn't as thorough as Candice. I didn't complain as I could see that home-boy was doing a great job. I was just accustomed to how things were previously handled. Life is all about adjustments though.

I hired a replacement for Darnell and I must say, that was working out very well. He was much more professional than Darnell and I could easily see myself promoting him to a higher position once he made it past his probation period.

Business was booming in early spring. The chitter-chatter had finally died down in the office about what happened between me, Candice and my wife and things were slowly getting back to normal. I was a little sad that Darnell and I hadn't patched things up and I no longer had my day one nigga to kick it with anymore, but as I said, life is about change.

Candice turned in her letter of resignation just as I instructed her to do and I was happy to have her out of my hair. Or at least I thought she was. I got to the office two days after Tierra had been attacked and was going through the mail that my assistant sat on my desk when I noticed I had a letter addressed to me but it didn't have a return address. I immediately recognized the handwriting from the many notes and kinky messages she would leave for me during our affair. I sat the envelope to the side and went through the rest of the mail before coming back to hers. I tapped on it as I pondered over whether or not I should open it. Butterflies filled my stomach as I expected some drama to be in the letter. I went on and tore open the envelope and pulled out the piece of paper she neatly folded and placed inside.

"Markel,

I guess you thought you wouldn't hear from me. And honestly I was hoping that I would hear from you. But I haven't. I can't believe you would use me the way that you did. I can't believe that you would lie to me and make me believe I was the woman you wanted to be with when really you treated me as your whore of the moment. I am not a toy to be played with and I will not just sit idly by while you spit on everything we've created together. I love you Markel, and I know you love me, too. I was too good of a woman to you just for you to turn on me the minute that bitch you call your wife found out about us. You think she is so perfect, little Miss Betty Home Maker, when really that bitch is just little Miss Betty Home Wrecker! You think you know your wife so well? You think she's so perfect? News flash! You don't know shit. You don't have a fucking clue as to what kind of a snake she really is. How about I clue you in? I would suggest you get a DNA test on both of your daughters because a little birdy told me at least one of them isn't yours. I know which one. But you don't. So who has the last laugh now, you black, adulterous, lying, cheating bastard! I fucking hate you and I hope you die!

I stared at the letter for a long time. Did this bitch just try to insinuate that my kids aren't my fucking kids?

Why is it that when a hoe gets thrown to the fucking curb, they resort to this Maury Povich bullshit? I got up and closed the door to my office and snatched the phone up from my desk. I was beyond pissed and was ready to light a fire in this smut-ass hoe. Her phone rang and rang and rang until it went to voicemail. Figures this little scared bitch wouldn't answer my calls. Too afraid to face me. She ought to be glad it's me she has to face and not Tierra because she definitely would have a bonafide ass whipping coming her way if I showed my wife this letter.

I called her phone three times, getting the same results. This fucking bitch... I decided to leave a voicemail.

"You had a lot of fucking mouth in that bullshit letter you sent me, you fucking smut-ass hoe. Bitch, it's one thing to get mad at me because I fucked and fleed you, but you brought my fucking kids into the bullshit? Bitch, you don't know a muthafucking thing about my wife or my kids, so save that fake ass mind game you're trying to play. You're mad because you were nothing

301

more than a bitch to slobber on my fucking dick and take it few times bent over. You used up ass, gutted-ass, slut-ass tramp. If I ever see you on the fucking streets, it's a fucking done bun for your ass. You fucked up bringing my kids into this shit. You better stay hiding wherever the fuck you are, because when I catch you, I'ma put an ass whipping on your bony ass that would make Ike Turner proud!" I slammed the phone down fuming but then immediately regretted leaving that message. God forgive me, but one thing I don't play with is my fucking kids. This bitch was crazy and definitely on some other time for this one.

My intercom beeped and I clicked it on to see what my assistant wanted. "Yes, Eric?"

"Mr. Davis, I have your wife on the line," Eric said to me.

"Okay, put her through." He patched her call to me and I immediately tried to mask my anger. Though I know Candice only said that shit to push my buttons, you can't say some shit like that to a man and he doesn't begin to wonder. "Hey, babe."

"Hey, honey. I was just calling to hear your voice. I was a little lonely in the house with the kids gone and taking a break from work. I hope I'm not interrupting you," Tierra purred through the phone. Her voice was always incredibly sexy and I could feel myself getting a hard-on despite how pissed I was at Candice.

"No you're not interrupting me. I'm just going through some mail and getting ready for my first client. Thursdays are always slow. How are you feeling?" I asked as I sat back down at my desk.

"I'm feeling better. Just kicking back in the bed and relaxing."

I was silent for a moment as I continued to think over what Candice said in her letter. Tierra could tell that something was wrong.

"Babe, is everything okay?" I heard Tierra ask me, snapping me out of my thoughts.

I shook my head. "Yeah, everything is fine. Listen, I have to go. I have a client coming in soon. Do you need me to pick you up anything on my way home?"

"Just some cookies n cream ice-cream, that's all. And some Oreo cookies. Yum!" Tierra giggled and I smiled.

"Okay babe, I got you. I'll see you tonight when I get home. Don't worry about cooking. Rest your pretty ass up because I'ma tear that ass up when I get in the house."

Tierra burst out laughing. "Mmm I love it when you talk dirty to me, Daddy," she said in a sexy voice.

"Yeah, Daddy Dick got something real nasty for you. I gotta go, babe. I'll order some pizzas and have them sent to the house for dinner. Just sign for them, alright?"

"Okay, babe. I love you," Tierra said in return.

"I love you too, babe." We disconnected the call and my mind wandered back to the letter. Candice didn't know me or Tierra like that to throw out some wild accusation like that, so I left it alone. But then I thought of who her father was; the notorious, bad-ass attorney, and my imagination began to get the best of me. Did he use whatever pull he has to do a background check on all of us and found out something I didn't know? Tierra said she knew all along that I was cheating on her back in the day. She didn't hesitate to get some pay back dick when she found out about me and Candice. Was she doing that all along back in the day and hid the shit better than I did? Could what Candice said really be true? As hard as I tried to push the thought out of my mind, I couldn't. She specifically said my daughters and not my son. I remember I stopped cheating on Tierra after we got married and had Tianna. So maybe she said my daughters specifically because Tierra knew I was being faithful and there was no need for her to cheat on me anymore but the whole time I was cheating on her, she was cheating on me too and slipped up but pushed Tianna and Tamia off as mine?

I was beginning to become upset with myself for letting that scrawny blonde haired bitch fuck with my head. I looked at a picture of Tamia and was positive that she looked like a younger version of my mother. She had her eyes and her smile but everything else was Tierra's. Tianna looked almost identical to Tierra except for her eyes. I looked at both of my daughters and closed my eyes. I was not going to let a scorned woman cause conflict in my family over a bullshit accusation without basis. These were my kids. Every single one of them. They were Davises. I was positive… I think I was positive…

25

Darnell

I had some money saved up and took some time off from work after resigning from the gig with Markel. I needed a break, shit. With all of the bullshit going on, I just needed to get away and take some time out for me.

I hadn't been in touch with Markel since I gave him my two weeks' notice. I deleted him and Tierra's frauding asses off of my Facebook as well as Candice. From now on, I was going to be more mindful of the company I was keeping.

I was seeing a new little honey dip that was turning out to be a good girl. I was taking things slow with her. I needed to make sure the bitch wasn't fucking my ex best friend, wasn't a lesbian or I wasn't going to be chilling on the couch with her one day and her fucking picture showed up on America's Most Wanted. I hadn't hit yet and wasn't pressed to either. She was a cool chick and I wanted to see how far things could go with her.

We were walking through the Art Museum looking over different sculptures and paintings. The new honey dip, Melissa, was heavy into art and it was cool for me to try something new. I heard about a new art exhibit that was going to be on display and decided to take her there on an afternoon date. There were some rowdy rugrats moving about on a school trip when I noticed Tianna in the crowd.

"Uncle D!" Tianna said excitedly as she ran over to me and gave me a big hug.

"Hey T-Money, what's popping, Shorty? I see you're in here with your little crew. You're on a class trip or something?" I asked her.

"Yeah, it's kinda lame though. Only thing I liked so far was running up the Rocky steps." We chuckled together.

"Melissa, this is my god-daughter Tianna; Tianna, this is my girlfriend, Melissa." I caught the way Melissa smiled when I referred to her as my girlfriend. Hey, what can I say? I'm maturing.

"Aw snap! Uncle D has a girlfriend. The world must be coming to a swift end," Tianna said as she covered her mouth to quiet her loud laughter. I chuckled with her. "What's up, Unc? How come you don't come around like that anymore?" Tianna asked me.

"Oh, my schedule's been real busy and I haven't had time, but I'll be around soon. How's your mom and dad?" I asked, though I honestly didn't give a shit. I hadn't matured that much.

"You don't talk to them?" Tianna asked with a raised eye-brow.

I hesitated. "I've been busy..."

Tianna stared at me for a moment and then nodded her head. "They're doing good. We're having a cookout for Memorial Day. You should bring Melissa and swing by."

"I'll think about it, Shorty."

"Ms. Davis, you know better than to wander off," Tianna's teacher said to her as she motioned for her to rejoin her class.

"Sorry Mrs. Snyder. This is my Uncle Darnell and I wanted to say hi." Tianna turned back to me with a long face. "I've gotta go."

"Okay, Lil Mama. I have your phone number, I'ma text you sometime," I said to her. She gave me a hug again but dropped her bag. We both bent over to get it at the same time when she saw the mark on my leg.

"Cool Unc! You have a mark on your leg just like mine," Tianna said as she pulled her sweatpants up to show me her birth mark that resembled mine. I turned my leg to the side a little and looked down at it.

"How about that...?" I murmured. "I guess that's why we both stay getting money." We chuckled together before her teacher called her again. Tianna gave me a pound and skipped over to join her classmates and teachers.

I looked back at my leg for a moment and then caught the way Melissa was looking at me. I threw my arm around her and we walked over to some paintings done by a local artist. I couldn't help glancing back at Tianna as she goofed around with her friends. I wonder...

26

Tierra

I had nodded off longer than I anticipated. I woke up to Tamia blowing on my eye lids. I fanned my hand in front of my face almost smacking her and she jumped back, giggling.

"Girl, you play too much. I almost knocked the hell outta you," I said to her as I rubbed my eyes. I stretched and sat up slowly. "What time is it?"

Tamia looked at her phone. "Almost 4:30pm," she replied. "Mom, this boy from my school asked me to the eighth grade dance. Can I go with him?"

I gave my daughter the side eye. "And what knuckle-head is this?"

Tamia chuckled. "He's not a knuckle-head, Mom."

"Unh huh. That's what all you little young thunder cats say."

"And you probably said the same thing about Daddy when y'all were my age," Tamia said with a half

310

grin. She saw the look that I gave her and her grin quickly disappeared. I decided to lighten up knowing that she was absolutely right. Her father was indeed a knuckle-head when we were growing up. But he was one of a kind. And now look at him. Look at us. I can't imagine loving any man the way I love him.

"I'll think about it, honey. Where's your sister?" I was getting up to make my way downstairs to make a sandwich. I was hungry as hell.

"She didn't get in yet. Mom, he is sooo cute. His name is Christian and he has the cutest hazel-green eyes. And he's sooo smart. He's like the smartest guy in our whole eighth grade class. And he's going to Central and plays basketball. He's a really great guy."

Tamia was really trying to sell me this young thunder cat. I would decide if his little young ass was all that and a bag of chips. Me and her father will tag team that ass Bad Boys 2 style like Will Smith and Martin Lawrence did that guy. Scared the hell outta his little young ass. *"Move bitch, get out the way, if I see you on the highway, get the fuck outta my way."* I found myself laughing out loud as I thought back to that movie. Tamia was looking at me as though I had lost my mind. It then dawned on me that Tamia said Tianna wasn't home.

"Wait a minute, what do you mean she didn't get in? You two get out at the same time, she wasn't on the school bus with you?" I asked Tamia as she followed me downstairs.

"Well, sometimes she catches the bus after me because of all of the sports and after school stuff she's into. And today she had that trip to the Art Museum with her class."

"They should've gotten back in time for her to make that bus. Basketball season is over and I don't recall there being any track practice today."

"I'm sure she's fine, Mom. Tianna mostly always comes in after me," Tamia said nonchalantly as she grabbed a handful of grapes out of the refrigerator and sat at the kitchen counter. I watched as she tossed them in the air and leaned her head back to catch them while I tapped my fingers on the counter. I dialed the school from my cell-phone.

"Hi, Mrs. Ginger. This is Tierra Davis, Tianna's mother. Was there track-practice today and it slipped my mind?"

"Hold on a second, let me check the after school schedule," the secretary said to me. I heard her shuffle through some papers as I waited patiently. "No, no track practice today and tomorrow due to the staff development meetings. She was dismissed regular time."

"Well, she wasn't on the first bus. Are you sure?" I asked as I started to worry a little.

"I'm positive, Mrs. Davis. If she missed the first bus, the second bus should be arriving with her soon."

"Okay, thanks Mrs. Ginger. Have a good evening." I disconnected the call and tapped my fingers on the counter as I began thinking some more.

"Is everything okay, Mom?" Tamia asked me.

"Let me text her to see where her little ass is. I swear she better be on that second bus or I'ma knock the hell out of her." I was more so in a slight panic mode for the simple fact that I knew someone had been watching me and I was just attacked a couple days before. Who knows if whoever that was who attacked me was watching my kids as well? Oh my God! What if they were? Markel and I were so busy thinking this maniac was just stalking me, we never even gave it a second thought that the bastard could have been stalking our

kids! I tried to remain calm as I didn't want to alarm
Tamia. I called Tianna first and she didn't answer.
Instead of leaving a voicemail, I decided to text her. I
was grateful that Markel had finally done what I asked
and gotten her a cell-phone too. And she knew the rule
was to never ignore our calls and text messages so she
better call right back or it's curtains for her. I sat the
phone down and waited patiently.

"Is your homework done?" I asked Tamia.

"I only had an article to read and a little bit of
Algebra to do. The school year is winding down, so
they're slacking off on the homework, thank God," she
giggled.

"Go do it while I wait for your sister." Tamia was
going to protest, but the look I gave her let her know to
keep her mouth closed and take her little ass upstairs like
I told her to. Fifteen minutes had gone by and Tianna
had not text back and did not call back either. I called
her phone again. Still no answer. Okay, now I was
worried. I decided to leave a voicemail.

"Tianna, this is your mother calling. I don't know
why you're not answering your phone or responding to
my text messages and I don't know why your ass wasn't

on that first bus with Tamia, but if your ass isn't in this house in the next five minutes, I'm going to give you the ass whipping you will remember me by, do you understand me?" I disconnected the call and began to pace the kitchen as my mind raced. Please don't let anything be wrong with my baby. This isn't like her at all. I checked the phone numerous times and she still didn't respond. I didn't like this shit at all. I decided to call my husband. It was after 5pm and Tianna still wasn't home.

I waited patiently for him to answer and to my surprise, it went to his voicemail also. What the hell was going on? Instead of leaving a voicemail, I decided to call his office to try to catch him before he left. His new assistant answered.

"Hey Eric, this is Tierra, Markel's wife. Did he leave yet?" What came out of Eric's mouth next almost made me lose my damn breath. It took a moment to register what he said.

"I'm sorry, Mrs. Davis. The police just came to the building and handcuffed Mr. Davis and took him out of here. I couldn't hear everything they said but if what I heard was correct, they took him to the police station under suspicion of murdering his former assistant, Candice."

"WHAT!?" I shrieked into the phone. "No, no way. No fucking way. Eric... no fucking way!" I was at a loss for words. Candice was dead! And Markel was a suspect!? And he was arrested. I must be fucking dreaming. Pinch me somebody, because this has to be a fucking dream.

"Mrs. Davis?" I heard Eric say to me. I was leaning onto the counter trying to catch my breath but before I knew it, I had burst into tears. "Ma'am I wish I had more information for you. Is there anything I can do?"

"No, I'll try to get in touch with someone at the police station and see what the hell is going on because this is definitely a mistake. My husband would never hurt anyone let alone kill them." I hung the phone up and put my hands to my face as I sobbed louder than I meant to.

"Mom, what's wrong?" Tamia asked sounding concerned. She put her arm over my shoulder and hugged me. "Is it Tianna? Is she okay?" Tamia asked me.

I swallowed past my hysteria and tried to regain my composure so I could answer my daughter. "It's not Tianna. It's your father."

316

"What happened to Dad!?" Tamia replied almost sounding frantic.

I didn't want to tell my daughter her father was a suspect in the murder of the whore he was recently fucking, so I kept it as brief as I could. "He's fine. There's just been a mix-up and the police took him in for questioning." Before I had a chance to say anything more, my phone went off with a text message from Tianna. Ugh, thank God. I opened the text and froze in terror. The world stopped and the room held the kind of silence that was so thick you could slice through it.

"What is it, Mom? Is that Dad or Tianna?" Tamia asked me as she tried to peep over my shoulder so she could see the phone. I clicked it off and sat it on the table.

"Tamia, go upstairs to your room, now."

"But Mom…"

"Go upstairs, now!!" I screamed at my child not meaning to. I saw when she jumped and immediately felt bad for yelling at her. She stormed out of the kitchen and went up to her room. My heart raced as I stared down at my phone and went back to the message.

There was a photo of my baby with duct tape around her mouth and her eyes. Even though her eyes were unseen, I could clearly see that she was terrified. Who was doing this? Who would take my baby? Xavier. It had to be him. He was sending me the letters; that was him who followed me the other day and attacked me. And now he has my baby. I grabbed the house phone so I could call the police when another text message came through on the phone. *"Don't even think about calling the cops, bitch. I know you're every fucking move. You call the cops or your husband, and this little bitch is dead."*

I slammed the phone down and put a trembling hand to my mouth. What the hell was I going to do? My husband was detained by the cops and someone had kidnapped our child. More than likely this was Xavier, pissed off that I ended the affair and broke things off with him. Trying to get back at Markel for hurting me was causing this ass-hole to hurt my child. Got damn it, why didn't I listen to my gut and get a gun regardless of what Markel said?

I wiped my face and took a deep breath as I tried to come up with a way to get in touch with the cops.

318

Another text message came through and I looked at it as butterflies filled my stomach.

"Open the door, bitch," the text message read.

I heard the doorbell and almost screamed. My heart pounded in my chest and I was positive that I was about to piss myself. I heard Tamia racing down the stairs.

"I got it, Mom!" she shouted.

I began to move from the kitchen quickly to stop Tamia. "Tamia, no! Don't open the door!" I screamed at her. I ran behind her to pull her away from the door but she was already unlocking it and opening it.

"Tee-Tee!" she screamed and was then silenced when Tianna was nudged forward and we both saw the chrome barrel of a pistol aimed at her head. We both could hear her whimpering. Her kidnapper stepped forward from the darkness and my mouth hit the fucking floor...

27

Markel

I remember hearing somewhere that fucking with White bitches will cause you more problems than a little bit. In all the years I had my flings with White women, Hispanics, even a few Asian cuties, I never had drama from anyone of them except for the White chicks. Now here I am, Markel Davis, CEO and lead Physical Therapist of one of the most prestigious Sports Therapy Centers in the country, sitting in a muthafucking jail cell because somebody decided this cock-gobbling whore was better off dead. Don't get me wrong, my heart goes out to the family and I am deeply remorseful. Despite that bullshit letter she sent me earlier, she was a good person and a nice young lady. I don't know the full details of her murder because I certainly didn't kill the bitch, but no one deserves to be killed at the hands of another person. I'm a lot of things, but murderer just ain't on my resume.

I was questioned excessively and the voicemail that I left her didn't help. At this point, they were doing a timeline from the time I left the voicemail until the time she was killed. Once that was established, they were able to get numerous statements from my employees and coworkers stating I was in the office at the time of the murder so it couldn't have been me. I thought that would have been enough. But these bastards were trying to insinuate that I had someone off her ass. W T F to that shit.

It was six hours before I was finally released with the warning that I would be brought back in for questioning and that in no way did this mean I was off the hook. I think for the simple fact that I was a successful Black man fucking a White chick who happened to turn up dead after the affair ended badly, they automatically saw me as guilty. Tell me this didn't sound like some Law and Order shit. I'm positive I saw an episode similar to this.

I retrieved my things and caught a cab back to the office. Before I started the car up so I could head home, I was going to call Tierra to apologize for being late and break the bad news to her when I saw I had a few missed calls from her. I checked my voicemail and one in particular caught my attention.

"Markel baby, please when you get this message, come home as soon as possible. Please. It's an emergency. We're in trouble. Tianna's been…" Tierra broke off sounding as though she was struggling with someone. I heard Tamia scream in the background not to shoot and then the call dropped.

Wait a fucking minute. What the hell…? I played the message two more times and then started the car. Whoever had been following my wife and threatening her was in my damn house with a gun and with my kids. I started to call the police but I had a feeling if whoever this was heard sirens or was suddenly surrounded by cops, they would do something desperate.

I was haul assing on I-95, damn near doing 90mph trying to get to my house. I didn't know what kind of situation I was getting ready to walk into, but I knew I had to do something to keep my family safe. I should have listened to Tierra when she suggested we get a gun. Trying not to be the typical nigga who needed to resort to gun slinging was haunting the shit outta me.

I wasn't sure if I was up against a crazed fan of Tierra's or someone she had an affair with that she was trying to keep a secret. That Xavier character who was married to the chick who tried to run her off the road popped in my head. Tierra insisted that nothing happened between the two of them, that it was just business. But nobody's wife is going to try to run a bitch off the road for nothing. There was more to that situation than she was telling me and I didn't appreciate being blindsided by the bullshit.

I made my way to the house and turned my headlights off just in case my wife and kids were being held in the den. I didn't want my lights to alarm whoever this was and have them react by licking off a few deadly rounds.

I stopped the car about half way up the driveway and cut the engine. My heart was pounding rapidly and loudly, so loudly that I was positive I could hear the shit thumping inside of my chest. My hands were sweating and my mouth was dry.

I was almost at the door when I could hear voices inside. One sounded like a very angry male and I could vaguely hear Tierra calmly trying to talk the person down. Before putting my hand on the door knob, I closed my eyes and said a quick prayer. *"God, give me the strength and ability to save my family even if it means losing my life to save theirs."* I twisted the door knob gently and pushed the door opened. It suddenly got quiet as though everyone in the house was waiting to see who the visitor was. My eyes searched the room quickly before stepping in and making my way into the den. Many scenarios and possibilities of what was going on and who was involved danced around in my head. But nothing could have prepared me for what I saw.

I stared at the man who casually had his hand around my daughter's throat and watched him as he aimed his gun at me. Our eyes locked and the silence in the room was deafening as I was trying to make my brain comprehend what my eyes were seeing. I stared at him for a long time in disbelief before I looked at my wife who was holding our oldest daughter Tamia, whose eyes were blood shot red from the endless flow of tears that continued to stream down her face. Tamia looked scared out of her mind, but Tierra was shockingly calm as though she had already accepted the situation for what it was- fucked up. Very fucked up in deed. But I couldn't accept it. No, I wouldn't accept it. It was no way in hell this shit was going down like this.

Yani

They say not to fear the enemy who attacks you, but the fake friend who hugs you. What the hell did I just walk into?

"Darnell, have you lost your muthafucking mind?!" I asked in as calm of a voice that I could muster, all things consider. The only thing stopping me from breaking his fucking neck was the fact that he had a gun to my daughter's head, though that was the exact reason why I wanted to break his fucking neck.

"Have I lost my mind?" Darnell said in a sinister voice that didn't sound anything like my day one nigga. "Oh no, I haven't lost my mind at all. More like, I'm seeing shit for what it is now and not what I want it to be."

Okay, now this nigga was talking in riddles. He definitely had lost his mind. "I don't know what the fuck you're talking about, but you need to take that gun..."

Darnell interrupted me. "Shut the fuck up! I didn't tell you to speak. I didn't ask you no muthafucking questions, nigga. When I want you to speak, I'll tell you to fucking speak, you got that shit?" he hissed in a dark and menacing tone.

I put my hands up to show I didn't mean any harm and in hopes that he would calm down. Tianna looked absolutely frightened and I could see where she had wet herself. She breathed heavily and looked at me with wide eyes as though she was pleading for me to save her.

"Darnell, please. Why are you doing this?" Tierra asked.

Darnell turned to her, pointing his gun. "You bitch, you definitely better shut your muthafucking mouth."

"Alright, Darnell. You're tripping on some bullshit right now. First off, get that fucking gun outta my wife's face, get your fucking hand from around my daughter's throat and talk to me man to man about what the fuck the problem is," I said to Darnell. I wasn't going to turn into a soft-ass pussy in the face of this nigga, gun or no fucking gun. If he had beef, we could handle this shit like fucking men; knuckle the fuck up.

"I'm tripping? No nigga, you're tripping. Always gotta be the fucking man. No, I'm the fucking man tonight. I'm the fucking man," he ranted. The look in his eyes was extremely cold; borderline evil. If looks could kill, he wouldn't have needed that gun. We all would've been dead.

Yani

"I been your boy for years, nigga. Fucking years! Soon as some pussy came into play, you turned into a straight up snake. First Tierra, then Candice. Yeah, y'all ain't know your poppa was a muthafucking rolling stone, sticking his dick in any bitch that would spread their legs for his punk-ass. He was a straight up hoe. But ya momma. Oh that bitch was an even bigger hoe," Darnell said as he looked down at Tierra. Though his mouth held a sarcastic smirk, his eyes held a look of contempt like someone who had been done terribly wrong.

I made a move towards Darnell, wanting to break his neck for disrespecting my wife the way he was doing in front of my kids. He pointed his gun back at me and Tamia screamed. Tierra threw her hand over her mouth, shushing her but I could hear her muffled pleas for Darnell not to hurt her daddy.

"Still defending this bitch after all these years. No wonder y'all asses still together. You fucked around on her and she defended you. She fucked around on you, you defended her. You just think you have the perfect fucking marriage Markel when the reality of it is all this time you've been living a fucking lie. Ask this bitch what's really real," Darnell said in a cocky tone. I looked at Tierra and then looked back at Darnell wondering what the hell he was talking about. So I asked him.

"What the fuck are you talking about, D?"

"Tell 'em, Tee. Tell this nigga how the whole sophomore year of college while he was running around with all of his side pussy how I was in y'all apartment beating that pussy up almost every fucking night. Tell this nigga how I used to bust that ass and had you begging for this dick, you tramp-hoe." Tierra looked from Darnell to me with tears in her eyes and then lowered her head in shame. "Yeah, bitch. Don't hang your muthafucking head now because that ain't the half. Tell this nigga why you really changed your number back then. Tell him why you was really hell bent on getting married when you got pregnant with y'all daughter…" Darnell knelt down next to Tianna and stroked the side of her face. She was visibly shaking. "My bad… I meant OUR daughter."

The room fell silent. I looked at Darnell and then looked at Tierra. Tierra put her hands to her face and began to weep. I thought back to the letter that I received from Candice and it started to become clear. Darnell killed Candice. He had her write that letter and send it to me because he knew that shit would fire me up enough to threaten her so when her body was found, I would be their first suspect since we previously had an affair. My homie, my ace, my day one nigga, set me the fuck up for murder. It then clicked in my head that he was the one following Tierra and had attacked her a couple nights before. There was no need to question why. It was simple. Darnell was in love with Tierra and thought they would be together after our fall out over my affair with Candice. When she didn't leave me, he snapped.

I stared at Tianna for a long time and then looked at Darnell. He still had that cocky smirk on his face and I wanted nothing more than to wipe that shit off with my fucking fist.

"You sonuva bitch," Tierra said as she looked up at him with fire in her eyes. "You jealous, sonuva bitch. You still never got over the fact that I chose Markel over you."

"Shut up, bitch," Darnell said acidly. He looked back at me. "I guess you don't believe me, huh nigga." He grabbed Tianna by her face and she whimpered louder.

"Look at her, Markel. You always said the eyes don't lie. Look at her. See the truth looking right back at you."

Not meaning to, I stared at Tianna. I looked at her and Darnell next to each other for what seemed like an eternity. I had never seen it before but at that moment, I saw it. Tianna didn't just look like Tierra. She looked like Tierra and Darnell. I never saw it before because I never questioned the paternity of my kids, and to me, my daughters always looked like Tierra.

Hate filled my heart at that moment as I felt the sting of an eleven year old lie. Before I knew it, I rushed Darnell. Tianna fell to the floor and Tierra and Tamia began screaming for us to stop.

Darnell and I tussled with gun back and forth as I tried to gain control of the gun while he tried to get enough leverage to shoot me. I wouldn't let up though. I could hear Tierra and Tamia screaming and begging for us to stop.

The gun went from being pointed upward to being pointed downward as I threw all of my weight into Darnell and began pushing him into the wall. I had both of my hands on his hand with the gun and he had his hand on my face, almost under my chin, pushing my head back to get me away. And then I heard a loud boom.

The gun discharged and Tierra screamed. There was a brief silence as it took a second to register that the gun had gone off. Darnell dropped the gun when Tierra screamed again.

"Tee-Tee!" she yelled as she scrambled over to our daughter. Tianna lay on floor as blood quickly began to stream out of her side. Tierra was hysterical as she cradled Tianna in her arms. I was frozen where I stood, unable to believe the chain of events that had occurred in the last 48 hours. The gun went off again snapping me out of my trance and I whirled into the direction that the gunshot came from. There stood Tamia holding the gun in both of her hands, standing over Darnell. Smoke rose from the barrel of the gun that my daughter held with shaky hands. She breathed heavily as she looked down at Darnell almost as though she was tempted to fire again. I quickly went over to her and put my hand over the gun, making her lower it before easing it from her hands.

"Is he dead?" she asked in a trembling voice. She stared down at him a moment longer before looking up at me, awaiting an answer.

"I don't know... I don't know. Call the ambulance now, Tamia. Now!" Tamia scrambled from the living room to get her phone and quickly dialed 9-1-1. I knelt down next to Tianna and took my shirt off so I could apply it to her wound. She was bleeding quickly. Way too quickly. I said to my wife again and again that she would be okay, our baby would okay, our little girl was a fighter and was strong and she was okay. I said those words again and again because I needed her to believe them. I needed our daughter to hear us fighting for her in hopes that she would keep fighting. And mostly I said it for my benefit as well.

Sirens blared in the silent night, bringing life to our once quiet and peaceful neighborhood. Flashing red and blue lights lit up the darkness of the streets as the cops and ambulance ascended up our drive-way. I needed this to be a nightmare that I was sure to wake up from any minute now...

Epilogue

Tierra

Heartbreak brought on by the sting of betrayal unveils a dark desire for revenge; Revenge to match my lover's deceit, forging a bond held together by lies to silence cries should the truth ever arise; One night of pleasure quickly turning into a lifetime of pain as caution is thrown to the wind and common sense no longer remains; My selfish desire to taste a forbidden fruit so sweet it quickly overshadowed its potential deceit; wrapping me in its treacherous, warm embrace, I felt safe to commit this act of sin. Justified in my eyes, little did I know of the chain of events I'd set into motion, making a hasty decision while being led by my emotions; Torn between the overwhelming power of love while overwhelmed by the power of hate; Stay or vacate? A question asked many times as the battle between my head and heart became more intense. This constant tug of war, back and forth as my conscience pays the expense. How wrong am I for doing what caused me so much hurt? How wrong am I for succumbing to my need to quench a self-righteous thirst? Torn between the overwhelming power of love while overwhelmed by the

333

power of hate. When a simple act of forgiveness could have spared me this fate…

I stared at the poem I had written in my journal. It had been a long time since I sat down and wrote a poem. I wrote poetry all the time as a teenager to help me cope with my father's murder. How different things would have been had I continued to use that as my outlet for my pain instead of running into the arms of my husband's best friend…

I stood in front of our bedroom mirror and stared at myself for a long time. It had been a while since I was able to look at my reflection in the mirror and meet my own gaze. I looked myself in the eyes no longer ashamed of the many lies I had told, no longer ashamed of the lie I was living. I just wish my lies did not cost a life.

Markel stood behind me and kissed the side of my mouth as I looked him in the eyes and he looked me in mine. I hated funerals and I was not ready for this day.

"I can't do this," I said to Markel as tears filled my eyes. I shook my head trying to blink back the tears to no avail. They fell like rain drops down my cheeks.

Yani

Markel shushed me and used his thumb to wipe away my tears. "You're the bravest, strongest woman I know. Your bravery and strength is why I married you. You can do this. We can do this. And we will do this together. Okay?" he said tenderly in my ear.

I nodded my head with a sniff and leaned my head against his. My husband was all that I wanted and needed in this world. When the truth came out about Tianna, I thought that would have destroyed us for sure. Instead it was the complete opposite. Markel took the blame saying in our therapy session that if he hadn't been out cheating on me in the first place, I never would have sought comfort in his best friend's arms.

I'd asked Markel if he wanted to get a DNA test for Tianna, but he said it was no point. In his heart she would always be his little girl and no blood test would change that.

I was amazed at the turn out for the funeral. You never know how much a person is loved unfortunately until they are gone. People from all over came to show our family support and pay their respects. I was eternally grateful for the outpouring of love, well wishes and sympathy.

At the cemetery, after the prayer had been read and final goodbyes had been said, we asked for a moment alone before the casket had been lowered into the grave.

Tamia did her best to stay strong and I couldn't help but admire her strength and courage as it mirrored my own. I took a hold of her hand as we stood in front of the grave in silence.

"Help me up, please?" Tianna said.

Markel and I along with Tamia, looked down at Tianna in shock as those were the first words that she had spoken since the night the gun had gone off and accidentally shot her.

"Baby, are you sure?" I asked her.

Tianna nodded her head. "Yes. Help me up, please?" she asked again.

I put an arm around her shoulder and Markel put an arm around her waist and we helped her stand from the wheel chair she was temporarily bound to. She slowly made her way to the casket. She reached out and ran her hands over the top.

"I'm not mad at you, Uncle D," she said softly. Markel sniffed and wiped the tears from his eyes from under his sun glasses. Tamia burst into tears next to me.

Yani

Though the cops ruled the shooting as self-defense, Tamia felt absolutely terrible that she had killed Markel's best friend. Though Tianna insists that she doesn't remember much of what happened while being held hostage and has no recollection of what Darnell alleged about being her father, Tamia heard everything and was sick with grief over the fact that not only had she shot and killed someone, but possibly killed her younger sister's father. And since Tianna had no memory of the horrible things that were said, we decided to never speak on what Darnell claimed again.

Tamia made her way over to Tianna and hugged her tightly, apologizing again and again. I stood back and shook my head feeling the weight of this tragedy on my shoulders. Regardless the fact that Markel was willing to take the responsibility for this, I felt the burden of this. Deep down I knew how Darnell felt about me and I never should have used him to get back at Markel.

We watched as Darnell's casket descended into his final resting place. I closed my eyes unable to look but unable to block out my husband's and children's cries. Tamia may have been the one to pull the trigger, but I was every bit as responsible for his death as she was, if not more. You never know what a person's mindset is and how quickly their feelings for a person can turn into an obsession if given just a small opening. And it doesn't take much for an obsession to turn deadly if that person is unable to obtain the object of their obsession as their possession. My husband and I played a dangerous game against each other and in the end, we all lost... R.I.P Darnell Jackson...

Made in the USA
Charleston, SC
15 June 2014